THE PINBALL THEORY OF APOCALYPSE

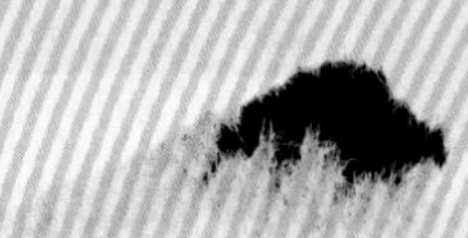

HARPER PERENNIAL

NEW YORK • LONDON • TORONTO • SYDNEY

THE PINBALL THEORY OF APOCALYPSE

Jonathan Selwood

F

HARPER PERENNIAL

P.S.™ is a trademark of HarperCollins Publishers.

HarperCollins books may be purchased for educational, business, or sales promotional use. For information please write: Special Markets Department, HarperCollins Publishers, 10 East 53rd Street, New York, NY 10022.

First edition

Designed by Jamie Kerner-Scott

Library of Congress Cataloging-in-Publication Data is available upon request.

ISBN: 978-0-06-117387-5
ISBN-10: 0-06-117387-8

07 08 09 10 11 ID/RRD 10 9 8 7 6 5 4 3 2 1

For Elizabeth

THE PINBALL THEORY OF APOCALYPSE

1

Just as I'm touching up the manic glint in Tom Cruise's eyes, another aftershock hits. I stumble back from the easel to try and keep from toppling over, but with the hardwood floor shifting violently in all three dimensions at once, it's like trying to cross a cobblestone street blind drunk in stiletto heels. Fortunately, a waist-high pile of old *Celeb* magazines breaks my fall.

The tremor ends just seconds after it starts, but a dry fog of lead paint dust continues to sift down from the ceiling. I wait a minute to make sure the ground isn't going to start moving again, then limp over to turn on the clock radio next to the futon couch. A male DJ's voice blares out in midstream.

" ... *is roughly equivalent to dropping a bowling ball off the Eiffel Tower. Please remember that phones should be used only in the case of an emergency, and not to call up the station and request the 'Earthquake Song' by the Little Girls. Let me also remind the two or three of you who haven't heard this before to refrain from firing up that crack pipe until you're absolutely positively sure you don't smell gas, to boil any tap water before drinking, and to slip on those Ugg boots before strolling over the broken glass and shards of jagged metal that most likely carpet your floor. . . . In other disaster news, one of our deservedly unpaid interns managed to spill wheat grass juice in all three CD players, so I'll be dipping into the vinyl vaults as we wait with bated breath for the always riveting Cal Tech report. . . .*"

X's "Los Angeles" starts crackling through the clock radio speaker. I turn up the volume, and take a minute to look around at the disaster that was once my apartment.

Dirty plates and cereal bowls are stacked everywhere, improvised ashtrays spill out over piles of old tabloid magazines, and layers of spattered paint cake the hardwood floor in a riot of clown colors. For the past two weeks I haven't seen my boyfriend, Javier, haven't checked the mail, haven't left the apartment for more than half an hour at a time. For the past week I've been too nauseated to eat anything but Trader Joe's pot stickers. And for the past three days I haven't changed out of my paint-spattered black T-shirt and jeans. All of this the result of my attempt to (in the words of my sociopathic art dealer Juan Dahlman) "launch my meteoric rise to fame."

Of course, in addition to the mess are the five new canvases that Dahlman plans to sell for a whopping fifty thousand dollars apiece come my opening Sunday afternoon (he claims Sunday afternoon is the new Thursday). Paintings I originally conceived as a satiric bayonet into the partially hydrogenated heart of contemporary society, but which my two-hundred-dollar-an-hour media training coach has reprogrammed me to call "transcendently kitschy."

Propped against my desk is Raphael's *Madonna and Child* with the original faces replaced by Britney Spears and her son Sean.

Hanging over the futon is David's *The Death of Marat* featuring a turbaned and bloody Kurt Cobain in the bathtub. And on the easel itself is *American Gothic* redone with a smiling Tom Cruise and Katie Holmes. As usual, the reproductions are technically flawless (with the exception, obviously, of the celebrity substitutions). I suppose if my new career as a sellout artist/media whore implodes, I can always move to Ibiza and become a professional forger.

The aftershock scattered my paintbrushes all over the floor, so I pick them up and carry them into the bathroom to clean. A new earthquake crack has appeared, running diagonally across the mildewed blue shower tile, but the two finished canvases I did with cobalt drier are still miraculously balanced on the towel rack. Placing the brushes in a coffee can on the soap dish ledge, I turn on the faucet. Rust-colored water spurts down into the basin, stops, then starts again with a shuddering of pipes, only to begin immediately pooling up from the paint-clogged drain. I shut the faucet back off, grab a bottle of "eco-friendly" drain cleaner from the ledge of the toilet, and pour the last of it in.

It takes a full minute of staring at the gaunt woman's face in the mirror above the sink for me to recognize it. My skin has drained from what I've always thought of as an SPF 15 pale to a tubercular pallor, my cheeks have sunken in painfully, and the dark circles under my eyes now match my black hair and T-shirt. Jesus, even my eyes themselves seem to be darkening.

The sink finally drains, and I'm about to begin cleaning the brushes, when there's a knock at the front door.

"Isabel? You in there? It's Chris," the superintendent calls from outside in the hall.

"Uh … yes." I head back into the living room and turn down the clock radio.

"You mind if I talk to you?"

"I'm kind of painting right now."

"No problem, I understand completely. I only wanted to tell you that I'll try and do something about the smell once they're finished with the structural tests."

Curiosity overwhelming creativity, I drop my brush back in the coffee can and walk over to the door, debating whether to open it.

"What structural tests?"

"Downstairs. You know, in the basement. They're checking the foundation."

I finally give in and tentatively open the door. Chris is in his late thirties, but suffers from an odd tapirlike downturn to his nose and face that emphasizes the severity of his receding hairline and makes him look far older. He's dressed in the usual blue jumpsuit and steel-toed Doc Martens work boots, but has an uncharacteristic cigarette sagging awkwardly out of the side of his mouth. Back in the '70s he was the child sidekick on a dreadful karate-themed TV show that, along with an alcoholic father who blew all of Chris's acting money in Vegas and jumped in front of an Amtrak, pretty much ruined his life. Knowing that once he gets in the apartment there's no telling when he'll leave or how many times he's going to ask me out for Ethiopian food, I hold the door only six inches ajar and try a more direct approach.

"What the hell are you talking about?"

"The smell."

"What smell?"

"That smell."

"Huh?"

"You can't smell that?" Chris raises a suspicious eyebrow.

"I smell … oh Christ!" I stumble back as the stench from the hallway hits me.

Chris uses my confusion to push through the door and into the center of the room. Holding the cigarette away from his face at arm's length, he inhales deeply through his tapir nose three times.

"It smells like paint in here! How'd you manage that?"

Trapped between wanting to shut the indescribably putrid smell out of my apartment and not wanting to shut myself in with Chris, I compromise by backing as far away from both the door and Chris as I can.

"Where the fuck is that coming from?" I try to breathe through my mouth.

"It's methane ... or at least I think it is. There's tar seeping up through a crack in the basement."

"Tar? It smells like ... Oh God!"

"Well, technically it's asphalt. It happened after the Northridge quake too, but this time it's way worse. I wouldn't be surprised if they condemn the building." Chris begins looking around the apartment for someplace to ash his cigarette.

I point to a squat Little League trophy next to the phone.

"I don't mean to be rude, but how can you live like this? It's unsanitary." He stubs out the butt of his cigarette and pulls a white and green pack out of the breast pocket of his jumpsuit. "Can I tempt you?"

"I didn't know you smoked." Deciding to ignore the "unsanitary" slur, I move to just within arm's reach and take one.

"Oh I don't usually smoke, it's just the ..." He gestures in the air with his hand at the smell.

"Unfiltered?" I pause momentarily, trying to figure out which end to put in my mouth.

"I swiped them from Larry Lichtman's apartment after the

coroner took him away. He had like twenty cartons." Chris pulls a box of strike-anywhere kitchen matches from his jumpsuit and offers me a light.

Forgetting that I haven't smoked or had a full meal in a week, I inhale deeply and nearly collapse when the rush of unfiltered tobacco hits my brain. Chris grabs both my arms and tries to steady me.

"Hello? Are you alright?" He leans in to look at me, the tapirlike slope to his face accentuated by the angle.

"Yep." I shake him off, almost collapse a second time, then manage to right myself with one hand on the bookshelf. "Just a little light-headed. What kind of cigarettes are these anyway?"

"Pura Indígena." He examines the pack. "They're made from that free-range tobacco."

"Free-range tobacco?"

"Well not free-range, but organic. Sort of like wild rice, you know, without all those pesticides and hybrids. I think they're made in Guatemala. . . ."

The first waves of another aftershock start and the painting of "*American Gothic* with Tom and Katie" promptly falls over, landing face-up on the hardwood floor. Chris reaches out to grab my arms again, but I sidestep him.

"Fine now," I cough.

"Really makes you wonder . . ." Chris looks up at the dark cracks flowering across the ceiling.

"Wonder what?" I brave another short drag of Pura Indígena.

"I'm no Cal Tech scientist or anything, but I've been working here since before the first Gulf War." He points to the ceiling cracks. "Wouldn't take more than a six point five to pancake this place like a parking garage. Splat!" He smacks one hand on top of the other in demonstration. "They'd need a spatula to get the bodies out."

"That's comforting."

"Yes, I suppose it is, in a way . . ." Chris nods pensively.

Before I can respond, my cell phone in the bedroom starts screaming Wagner's "Ride of the Valkyries." My boyfriend Javier downloaded the ringtone a month ago as a joke, then ran off to work without fixing it (he works crazy hours as a personal chef). Despite reading and rereading the online help tutorial at least five times, I still haven't figured out how to change it back to a simple bleep.

"I better get that."

"Sure." He nods, but doesn't budge.

I head into the bedroom and find the phone under a pile of dirty laundry. Unfortunately, the number that comes up on the screen is not Javier's, nor even my mother's (who consistently ignores the "emergency calls only" pleas on the radio), but that of my art dealer, Dahlman.

I take a deep breath, then slowly let it out before answering.

"Hey, Dahlman."

"*AHHHHHHH!!!!*" he responds with his trademark primal scream, something my mother says he's been doing since undergoing unaccredited Gestalt therapy in the mid-'70s. Even though I'm expecting it, it's still disconcerting. "*Isabel, babe, how are you?*"

"Okay, I guess."

"*Well, prepare to be a whole fuck of a lot better than okay! Some dot-com dork just walked in here and bought seven goddamn paintings!*"

"That's great."

I realize too late that my words lack the appropriate exclamation points of enthusiasm.

"Don't you fucking start with me, Isabel!"

"I'm not starting with you."

"Good. Then shut your ungrateful pie hole and meet me at Musso's in ten minutes. I've got another ad campaign for you."

Dahlman's recently taken it upon himself to not only show my work at his gallery, but to be my de facto agent as well. In the past three months (in addition to several photo shoots and at least a dozen interviews), he's gotten my paintings into a Japanese cosmetics campaign and a ridiculous Dominican rum billboard ad, the latter of which made the fatal marketing error of using a literal translation from the Spanish for its English language slogan "Chupacabra rum! It bites!"

"I have to take a shower first." I stall for time, fearful of what he's come up with this time.

"TEN MINUTES!!!" He hangs up.

Dahlman's Argentinean sense of time would make him two hours late to his own firing squad, so I'm not really in a rush, but when I head back into the living room I do my best to appear flustered. Of course, Chris fails to get the message, and there's an awkward pause as I wait for him to leave and he desperately tries to think of a reason to stay. My cat, Jello, peeks out from around the kitchen door to see who's here, takes a sniff at the air, and retreats back into the kitchen.

"You really should smile more." Chris falls back on the classic.

"I don't smile." Which is simply the truth.

Despite the paint fumes and cigarette smoke, the smell from the hallway is starting to overwhelm the room. No wonder Jello fled. Before I can make a comment about needing to get back to work, Chris's attention drifts to the fallen canvas of "*American Gothic* with Tom and Katie."

"This is what you're working on now?" He leans his face in close to examine the canvas, then steps back, closes one eye, and holds his thumb up to it.

"I don't usually show my work before it's dry." I move to try and block his view.

"No no ... It's good. You really nailed his creepy eyeball thing." Chris nods his head in approval. "How long have you been at this?"

"This painting?"

"No, I mean did you start painting in college, or was it one of those things you've been doing as long as you can remember?"

"Thanks for the smoke, Chris, but I really need to take a shower right now."

"You know ... " He leans in again to examine the painting over my shoulder. "I don't know much about art, but I think this is even better than the Cameron Diaz one you painted for that cosmetics campaign."

"I didn't paint it for the campaign. They bought the rights to use it in their ads." I give up on any subtleties and start physically pushing him towards the door.

"Never thought of being a painter myself. Don't have any...." He makes a futile circle in the air with his cigarette hand "... talent."

I open the door with one hand while propelling him forward with the other.

"Yeah, well, I better go see if I can find some Glade PlugIns to cover up that smell." He steps partway through the doorframe, then turns back. "Hey, I don't suppose you want to try that new Ethiopian place on San Vicente?"

"Chris, I have a boyfriend. Remember?"

"Right … right … but he's working for Mirabel Matamoros these days, isn't he?" Chris asks with a wink, referring to the sixteen-year-old Latina pop singer who recently hired Javier as her full-time chef. "Did you know she's actually a Mormon? She uses a speech coach to fake the Spanish accent."

"What did you mean by that?"

"I mean she's totally Latter-day Saint. Born and raised in Salt Lake City."

"No, what did you mean by that wink?"

Chris gives me a funny look (which comes across as doubly odd, since he's already pretty funny-looking to begin with).

"Nothing." He shakes his head. "I just thought … well, he hasn't been around much lately. Not to be critical or anything, but you should hang out with friends more."

"No critique taken."

"Sure I can't tempt you with a platter of kitfo? The whole waif thing …" He looks me up and down. "It's dead. A little raw beef simmered in clarified butter would go a long way towards bulking you up for the winter."

I force a smile, then quickly close and dead-bolt the door.

Despite the door being closed, the putrid smell from the hallway is getting stronger. I walk into the bathroom, toss the butt of my cigarette into the toilet, and turn on the shower. Of course, the water comes out rust brown, but at least the drain works, and after a minute or so, it begins to run clear. Momentarily distracted by the "*Raft of the Medusa* with the Original Cast of *Survivor*" resting on the towel rack, I forget to avoid looking in the mirror, and the glimpsed reflection of my emaciated body as I pull off my T-shirt makes me wince. Chris's comment about the "waif look" is right—my formerly snug jeans won't stay up without a belt, my ribs are jutting out above my abdomen like an accordion, and my breasts have retreated to those of a twelve-year-old.

In the past three months, I've been transformed from an unknown hack into Dahlman's vision of an "It Girl" artist, been given a solo show at possibly the biggest gallery in LA, and have made over a hundred thousand dollars in advertising deals alone. Yet I'm so stressed out, I can barely eat.

I give new meaning to the term "starving artist."

2

I'm not sure if there is a "normal" way for artists to suddenly rise to fame, but my own story strikes me as utterly random.

Five years ago, after slogging through an undistinguished undergraduate degree in studio art at UC Santa Cruz, I proudly hung the best of my David Hockney knockoffs (which at that time I more or less specialized in) for my senior art show. Despite the overtly hostile critiques I'd been receiving in class, I still had the naïve hope that the show would somehow be well-received and launch my career as a painter (or at least help me get into an MFA program). However, as anyone but an idealistic idiot like myself could have predicted, the show was not well-received. In fact, it was a fucking disaster. I spent most of the evening hiding in the corner with a Dixie cup of jug wine while local wannabe art aficionados gathered in semicircles around my paintings and openly joked about whether or not I should be sent to Guantánamo for my crimes against art.

The next day, the head of the art department called me into his office. He sighed two or three times for effect, and then pointed out the obvious—that my work not only failed to impress the people at my senior show, but that most of the art teachers hated it too. Of course, hearing this from my favorite professor in all the four years I'd spent in college made me break down and cry like a fucking moron. This was during the peak of another politically correct inquisition, so he was only able to pass the Kleenex and give me an awkward pat on the shoulder, before handing me the business card of a Beverly Hills interior designer. "My ex-wife Cheryl," he said by way of explanation. "She could really use someone with your technical abilities."

After graduating, I spent a miserable six months as an office temp in San Francisco, before reluctantly moving back in with my parents down in Hollywood and calling my professor's ex-wife. Apparently Cheryl was still on good terms with him, because she hired me over the phone to work as what she called a "fine art facsimilist." There is, evidently, a surprisingly large percentage of the wealthy (but not quite Sotheby's auction–wealthy) who want to fill their atrocious McMansions with famous artwork that they can't actually afford. Forgoing the ubiquitous poster reproduction of Monet's *Water Lilies*, they hire someone to actually paint an identical copy—and that someone turned out to be me. My technical ability (coupled I suppose with my temporarily derailed drive for self-expression) made me the ideal choice for the job. Cheryl had already lost two previous freelance "fine art facsimilists" in the past year, so she paid me handsomely—up to twenty-five bucks an hour, depending on the level of difficulty. The jobs were mostly the lesser-known works of the Impressionists (just unfamous enough for the client's friends to think they might be genuine), but

I copied everything from El Greco to Jasper Johns. Moving out of my parents' house and into this apartment, I managed to work more or less full-time at it, and streamlined the process until I was pumping out one or two "masterpieces" a month. It really wasn't so bad, except for the nagging voice in the back of my head telling me to blow out the pilot light and jam my head in the oven.

It took almost five years, but my lucky break finally arrived in the form of a gay couple who, obsessed with Dan Brown's novel *The Da Vinci Code*, hired Cheryl to turn their Studio City faux Southern Plantation nightmare into a Tuscan villa. When she suggested the obvious choice of a *Mona Lisa* reproduction for the living room, the couple countered with the novel idea of a *Mona Lisa* with the face switched to Cher's. At first I was a little apprehensive, but a Google image search online brought up a suitable headshot, and the substitution turned out to be a piece of cake. Because of construction delays on the Tuscan villa, *Mona Lisa/Cher* was hanging in my apartment for three months before they finally picked it up, and the more I looked at it, the more I liked it. The initial campiness quickly wore off, and the surgical blankness of Cher's face obscuring da Vinci's Renaissance masterpiece seemed to say something truly disturbing about the modern world.

Between the shower and searching for my keys, it takes me almost an hour before I'm ready to leave for my meeting with Dahlman at Musso's.

When I finally step out of my apartment and into the second-floor hallway, the stench seems to skip my nose altogether and seep right through my skull. Something primitive in my brain locks my lungs and shuts off my breath as if I'd just plunged underwater.

Without any conscious will, I find myself sprinting down the stairs, past the blue blur of Chris's jumpsuit, and out of the building. I'm halfway across the street before my lungs finally start up again and begin gasping for fresh (or at least pleasantly smoggy) air. A second later, the front door to the San Maximón Arms slams shut behind me and cuts off Chris's laughter.

South Orange Grove Avenue is a standard strip of asphalt with two-story white stucco apartment buildings lining either side. Even though most of the buildings are old by LA standards, it's still more familiar for its similarity to all the adjoining streets than for any distinctive landmarks. The main reason I decided to move into this south-of-Wilshire-one-block-east-of-La-Brea neighborhood (which I'm sure has an actual name, although I've never heard anyone use it) is because it's just far enough from where my parents live in Hollywood to keep my mother from popping over while I'm trying to paint. With the money supposedly about to flood in from my "meteoric rise to fame," everyone (that being Dahlman, Javier, and my mother) keeps suggesting I move somewhere more artistically fashionable, but I kind of like living in the middle of nowhere—even if that nowhere happens to be right smack in the center of a city pushing fifteen million people. When my breath finally slows and I blink away the tears in my eyes, I wave to the Trinidadian guy who always walks his Shetland sheepdog at this time, and notice an odd pinkish-brown glow overhead, as if the smog-enhanced LA sunset has come a few hours early.

Even after fourteen days of inactivity, my primer black '73 Nova starts immediately. In the two years since I bought it for five hundred dollars off the stripper who used to live in the apartment across the hall, it has never once had a problem (despite the fact that I haven't even raised the hood, much less changed the oil). With an odometer that's already flipped over at least twice, the car is downright miraculous.

While giving the engine a chance to warm, I punch through the preset buttons on the radio (the tuning knob fell off six months ago, and you need a pair of pliers to get anything else). Irritatingly enough, all five stations are now playing a prerecorded evacuation message for people fleeing a wildfire in Silverlake caused by one of the aftershocks, and I'm forced to grope under the passenger seat for my one flea market eight-track tape. Like just about everyone else in Southern California, I've come to accept the relentless stream of natural disasters as a part of life, and pay attention only to those that directly affect me. I pull a blind U-turn from the curb, pop in the tape, and Debbie Harry begins to sing, slightly warbled, from the two front speakers.

I put on my sunglasses.

For a city that's supposed to be my own—that I was born and raised in—Los Angeles has an exceptionally foreign look. The exotic palm trees bulge obscenely out of urban concrete, the giant billboards explode with blockbuster movies that I'll never bother to see, and the low white retrofitted buildings spill out over the desert floor with flimsy impermanence. Stucco fronts of stores and restaurants change so fast that even streets I've driven hundreds of times before can suddenly become totally unfamiliar, forcing me to pull out the inch-thick *Thomas Guide* map and navigate like a tourist through my own neighborhood. Even when I am confronted with an enduring landmark—like the Chinese Theatre or the Capitol Records building—it serves less to recall the past than to mark its extinction.

Traffic's unusually light, and I manage to make it to Musso & Frank's in under twenty minutes. The goateed parking attendant acknowledges my presence with a slight nod, but doesn't come over, so I have to walk up and get a ticket.

Musso's itself hasn't changed since Faulkner and Fitzgerald ate here in the 1930s (during their own days of abject artistic prostitution), but the constant turnover in its entertainment industry patrons keeps the place surprisingly lively. I make a quick pass through the booths of the "old" room to make sure Dahlman hasn't gotten a table, then head around to the bar in the "new" room (which is still a lot older than I am). Despite the early-bird hour, most of the tables are filled, but of course Dahlman isn't there either. Just the smell of real hot food in the air is making me feel faint, so in spite of my nervous stomach I go ahead and order the sand dabs.

The bartender writes down the order, but then just stands there making strange jerking movements with his eyes and neck. Still adjusting to the world outside of my apartment, I stare dumbly at him for half a minute, before realizing that he's signaling for me to look at something. Unlike the tables, the bar is almost empty of patrons, and I quickly follow his eyes to an obese Mexican man sitting at the far stool by the kitchen. With his short black bowl-cut hair, tight pink tank top, and stretched iridescent yellow bike shorts, he strikes me as some kind of exotic bird. After watching for a moment, I realize that he's crying.

"He's been like that since lunch," the bartender whispers to me. "Hasn't ordered a thing."

"What's wrong with him?"

"Every day he comes in smiling and drinks Cuba libres. You know, we talk. He's a regular. And then all of a sudden he comes in dressed like this. I think it's his *corazón* … you know, his heart. It's broke."

"He got dumped?"

"No no . . . a clogged aorta or something." The bartender shrugs and heads off to put my order in at the kitchen.

Not wanting to stare at a man while he's crying, I glance around the room again and notice a group of vaguely familiar-looking young actors in the corner booth. One of them catches me looking, and flashes the most arrogant smile I've ever seen—he actually tilts his head back to raise his nose up in the air. Almost without thinking, I counter his arrogant-asshole smile by gesturing that he has something caught in his teeth. The smile vanishes and a look of horror crosses his face. I grab a cocktail straw off the bar and mime cleaning my teeth with a toothpick. The horror turns to panic as he checks the room for lurking paparazzi, and then uses his napkin for cover while he attempts to clean his teeth with a thumbnail.

I quickly swivel back to the bar so he can't see me laughing, and to my surprise, the bartender returns with a giant porterhouse steak smothered in butter. "Here."

"Actually, I ordered the sand dabs."

"The writer who ordered this got a call from Miramax and took off running. You're not a screenwriter, are you?"

"No."

"I fucking hate writers." He drops the steak in front of me and starts to walk away.

"But I ordered the sand dabs," I call after him.

"Sand dabs are baby food." He eyeballs me up and down. "You need red meat. Besides, it's free."

I look down at the steak. It's so rare that it's bleeding all over the plate, but somehow, despite my upset stomach, it looks phenomenally good. The "free" part doesn't hurt either.

"Alright. Thanks."

When I first started painting what I like to call the "Subbing Celebrities" series, my perennially peppy mother, who had never been able to muster more than a confused nod at my earlier work, was ecstatic. She showed up unannounced one Tuesday morning and dragged me over to West Hollywood to meet a former-bottomfeeder-music-talent-agent-turned-gallery-owner who she knew from back in her free-love commune days and who owed her a favor. Since the only "gallery" experience I'd ever had was a single painting hanging next to the restroom in a Santa Cruz coffee house (the guilt-induced result of a one-night stand with the assistant manager), Dahlman came as something of a shock. Before my mother could even introduce me, he brought out the tape measure and took my measurements. Then, rubbing his chin as if in deep thought, he sent off his assistant to buy me a Wonderbra.

"You'll do." He nodded twice. "But if you ever cross me, I will gut you like a fucking emu! Understand?"

"Uh … okay."

Dahlman got on the speakerphone, and for the next two hours I found myself sitting mutely through a meeting with Dahlman's other assistant, a PR guy, a web designer, and not one, but *two* stylists. Despite finding Dahlman utterly repulsive in both personality and appearance (knowing that he'd probably had unwashed hippie-sex with my mother didn't help), I was then bullied into letting him come over to my apartment to see my work—apparently years of representing musical "talent" had taught Dahlman to simply outshout people into submission. When he walked in the door and saw my "Martha Stewart as *The Scream*," he let out his own trademark primal scream (which scared the living shit out of me) and produced a half-sneer/half-grimace that my mother later informed me was his version of a smile.

"How many of those can you pump out in a month?" He pointed at *Martha*.

"One or two."

"Better make it three or four. Your debut show is less than fourteen weeks away."

"Are you serious?"

"That, my petite-breasted friend, is fucking twenty-four-karat gold-plated gold." He grabbed his crotch and tugged for emphasis. "I take fifty percent, and remember, I'm only representing you because of your mom."

By the time Dahlman finally shows up at Musso's, I'm halfway done with the porterhouse. It's fantastic. I can't remember the last time I just ate a giant slab of meat like this.

"What the fuck are you doing in the 'new' room?" he shouts loud enough for the whole restaurant to hear.

My excitement over the porterhouse is immediately tempered by the way his stick legs, barrel chest, and thinning gray ponytail amplifies the bloated feeling in my newly stretched stomach. He has the sleazy pansexual look of a failed pornographer, and recalling the fact that he's never openly hit on me only makes me more repulsed. A cell phone earpiece still attached to his head, he waddles towards me like a giant ground sloth.

"You're late," I counter.

"My Porsche got pancaked. I parked it in one of those multilevel garages, and the whole thing came down in an aftershock yesterday. They'll need the jaws of life to get it out." Dahlman sits down on the stool next to me and orders a Kahlúa on the rocks. "Isabel darling, I'm going to make you more famous than Basquiat." He pulls out a purple check and waves it in front of my eyes just long enough for me to see that it's for three hundred and fifty thousand dollars.

"Mine?" I reach for it, but he puts it back in his pocket.

"Alex Tzu." He sips his Kahlúa with his pinky finger raised like an old lady taking tea. "The dot-com dork. The guy's fucking in love with you. Thinks you're the next Cassius Coolidge. He even wants you to come over to a cocktail party at his house tonight."

Before I can ask him who Cassius Coolidge is, he stabs an enraged finger at me.

"Jesus Christ, Isabel! Would it kill you to smile once in a while? You look positively lugubrious."

"I'm an artist, I don't have to smile."

"Then how about a tit job? I could triple your sales with a C-cup." He sips again at his Kahlúa, then finally removes the cell phone earpiece and pockets it.

"No."

"I get you the cover of the *Sunday Calendar* section, and this is how you treat me?"

"I got the cover?"

"No, *I* got the cover ... for you."

"That's great!" Excitement temporarily overtakes my repulsion.

"Well, think about it, okay? I mean, the tit job." He cups his hands to demonstrate the heft breast implants would give me.

"I'm not getting a tit job."

"Fine, fuck you." Dahlman shakes his head. "But I don't want to hear any shit when it comes to this..."

He pulls a torn magazine ad from his back pocket and smooths it out on the bar. It features a middle-aged female naval officer standing on the deck of an aircraft carrier. She's wearing dress whites and has a half-smiling look of authority that somehow seems to suggest more of a dominatrix than a commanding officer. In bold letters across the top it says "**LOOSE LIPS SINK SHIPS!**" and then below "Have you talked to your doctor about VR?" There's no text at all to explain what it is that's actually being advertised.

"I don't get it," I admit.

"Okay, how about this, then …"

Dahlman pulls a second and far more crumpled magazine ad out of his front pocket and again smooths it on the bar. This one is even more bizarre, with a line of high school boys in tuxedos in the process of pinning corsages on their prom dates. The prom dates are also all high school–aged, with the exception of one—a giggling woman with gray hair who must be at least sixty. This time the copy reads "**YOUTH IS WASTED ON THE YOUNG!**" but with the same "Have you talked to your doctor about VR?" printed below. For the life of me, I can't figure out the meaning of either of the two ads.

"I still don't get it." I shake my head. "What the hell does 'VR' stand for?"

"*Vaginal rejuvenation.*"

"Vaginal what?"

"It's the fucking future of plastic surgery, baby. A little clitoral resurfacing here, an aesthetic snip of the meat flaps there, and you're ready to spread for *Playboy*. In ten years it'll be bigger than liposuction." His face contorts into the half-sneer/half-grimace that he uses instead of a smile.

I'm actually struck dumb by this as my brain finally deciphers the message the two ads are trying to convey.

"Get this, they're offering a quarter mil for TV, billboard, magazine, Internet … the works," Dahlman continues. "That's a quarter of a million dollars for less than a week's work. It's fucking juicy."

"Let me get this straight. You want … you want me to do an ad for vaginal rejuvenation?" I ask, incredulously.

"Not just one ad, a whole fucking series. You see, they're using *real* people in these ads. It's part of a strategy to mainstream the idea. You know, like those football players they got to hock Viagra. I mean this naval officer…." He points to the ad lying on the bar. " … is like a *real* naval officer fighting in Iraq. And this old grandma woman…." He points to the other ad. " … is like a *real* old grandma. She even—"

"No way," I finally recover enough to cut him off.

"What are you talking about? For Christ's sake, they've even come up with a tag line for you: *Beauty Is in the Eye of the Beholder*. Picture yourself painting at the easel while a whole troupe of bowtie-clad Chippendale dancers—"

"Dahlman!" I cut him off again. "I don't care what they're paying. There's nothing wrong with my vagina, and there is no fucking way I'm getting surgery."

"Don't be silly. You don't have to actually *have* the surgery. You just need to make people *think* you've had the surgery."

"NO!" I crumple up the ads and throw them at him for emphasis.

Dahlman leaps off the stool so suddenly that for a second I think he's going to hit me, but instead waves at the group of vaguely familiar-looking young actors in the corner booth.

"Isabel, don't make me break your thumbs, because I'll do it."

"If you break my thumbs, I won't be able to paint anymore."

"You can paint with your mouth like a quadriplegic. It'll add a human interest side to your mystique."

"I'm not doing it."

"As I mentioned, we stand to make a quarter million off this ad campaign, so obviously I'm going to win this argument, but since I have another engagement to attend, let's continue this later." He checks his watch. "That said, you goddamn motherfucking better be at this party tonight." He hands me Alex Tzu's address written on the back of a Dahlman Gallery card. "*Forbes* says the guy's thrown away almost a billion dollars on random shit in the last four years, and he ain't even close to slowing down. Besides, the *Times* photographer's gonna be there to get the *Calendar* cover photo. He wants to shoot you cinema verité style."

"You know I hate these things."

"Don't fuck me on this, Isabel! Don't you fuck me!" he suddenly screams.

People all over the restaurant are turning around in their booths to look.

"Okay. I'll be there." I try my best to calm him down.

"Good." Dahlman's voice immediately drops back to normal. "Now give me a ride over to Paramount." He hops up and starts heading for the door.

"What about your bill?" I call after him.

"Hey, you're the famous artist, aren't you?" He leaves without looking back.

Having heard everything, the bartender comes over with the Kahlúa bill, and I pay it.

"Sorry," for some reason I apologize to the obese Mexican guy with the broken heart.

He shrugs.

Another aftershock hits just as I step out the door of Musso's, and I instinctively jump back to get away from the windows. While I watch, a crack starting only a few inches from me snakes its way through the parking lot asphalt and up the stucco wall of the building next door. By the time the shock ends, it's at least an inch wide at my feet.

I look up at the goateed parking lot attendant, who at first shrugs his shoulders with a smile, but then stops smiling and looks at me intensely. He lifts his right index finger to his right cheek and pulls it down in a gesture that makes his eyeball appear much larger, then points with the same finger directly at me.

"*Mucho ojo,*" he says in Spanish.

I can tell the gesture is some kind of warning, but I'm not sure what it means, and it kind of creeps me out.

"Are you coming?" Dahlman screams at me from where he's talking on his cell phone next to the Nova.

I walk over, unlock the driver's side door, and get in, only to have Dahlman appear at my window.

"Move over, I'm driving."

"But it's my car!"

"You're so possessive. You really need to deal with that." He uses his barrel chest to force me into the passenger seat.

With Dahlman driving the Nova like he's in the chase scene from *Bullitt*, we peel out of the parking lot and onto Hollywood Boulevard. Homeless teens and overweight Midwestern tourists alike turn to look. Between the roar of the engine and the squeal of the tires, I can barely hear my cell phone playing "Ride of the Valkyries."

"Hi, Mom," I answer when Dahlman is finally forced to stop at a light.

"That was one big aftershock! Are you alright?"

"Not really. Dahlman's driving my Nova like a maniac."

"You let him drive?"

"It's not like I had much of a choice."

"Oh! By the way, that reminds me. Your aunt Bridget tried to log onto www.isabelraven.com, but that Internet blocker program she put on the computer to keep her husband from downloading porn won't let her connect. I bet it's all those nude pictures of you in Joshua Tree. You should tell Dahlman."

"There are nude pictures of me on my Web site?" I direct the question at Dahlman, but my mother hears too.

"Of course not." He floors it as the light changes.

"You know, the ones Toby took during your spring break," my mother replies. Toby was my freshman year Leica camera–obsessed boyfriend, who after feeding me half a bag of mushrooms managed to convince me to pose naked for him on our camping trip to Joshua Tree. But being a nice guy, he gave me not only the

prints, but also the negatives when we broke up a month later.

"How the hell did Dahlman get those?"

Dahlman pretends to concentrate on the road. Actually, considering we're doing almost sixty in a thirty-five zone with heavy traffic, it's possible he really is concentrating.

"They were in that box of photos I found in the garage. Dahlman called me last week and asked if I had any good photos of you, and—"

"You gave him naked photos of me?"

"No, honey, you don't understand. The photos are really very tasteful." As usual, she misses the point entirely.

We reach the Bronson entrance to Paramount Studios, and Dahlman pulls over on the wrong side of the road, using the horn to terrify the "live studio audience" line that's drifted out into the street while waiting to get into a late taping.

"Mom, I have to go." I hang up and turn to Dahlman. "You put naked pictures of me on the Internet?"

"Hey, those pictures quintupled the number of hits on your Web site."

"I was seventeen in those pictures! That's like child pornography!"

"You weren't seventeen." Dahlman actually looks nervous. "Your mom said you were a freshman in college."

"A seventeen-year-old freshman! I skipped kindergarten!"

"Really?"

"Really!"

"Fine." He sighs. "If you're going to be that way, I'll take them off. But we're going to have to shoot some more. I know a guy who does classy work. He's not cheap, but he's a total pro—used to shoot for *Barely Legal*."

"I can't fucking believe you!"

"Aren't you going to ask me what I'm doing at Paramount?" he asks, trying to deflect further comment.

"No."

"I'm pitching your life story."

"You don't know my life story."

"That's why it's a 'based on' as opposed to a 'told to.'"

"Why the hell would anyone want to make a movie about my life?"

"Not just anyone, babe. We're talking Lindsay fucking Lohan."

"You're pitching to Lindsay Lohan?"

"Of course not. But word is, she creamed her shorts over that Toulouse-Lautrec you did of her." Dahlman climbs out. "Hey, by the way, I noticed you never signed the contract I sent you to legally make me your agent. There's another copy down at the gallery, so go down and sign it right now."

"Nobody uses their gallery owner as their agent. It's almost as ludicrous as putting naked photos of your artists up on their Web sites."

"Back to the photos again. You're a fucking broken record, you know that? Anyway, I don't care what 'nobody' does. I care what *you* do. If I'm going to bust my ass getting you advertising deals, I want more than an implied verbal contract."

"No. I won't sign it."

It's really the naked pictures that I'm objecting to, but for some reason this is where I draw the line. However, a furtive glance at Dahlman's face to see how he's taking it reveals that the line isn't going to stay drawn long.

"ARE YOU CALLING ME AN ASS CLOWN?" he screams.

"I—"

"You're calling me an *ass clown*, aren't you?"

"I don't even know what an ass clown is."

"This isn't a goddamn game! I will gut you like a fucking emu!"

"Alright! I'll sign the contract. Just get out of my car, will you?"

"Back on that possessive trip again." He shakes his head.

4

I'm back in the Nova and stuck in traffic on my way to Dahlman's Melrose gallery when the fist of my mind finally unclenches and I let out a stream of vaguely pertinent obscenities. Dahlman always has this effect on me. He's so overwhelming in person that I more or less shut down completely around him, bottling everything up to uncork later at a suitably inappropriate time. My mother once told me that back in the commune days they actually had a young Charles Manson crash with them for a couple of weeks, and I wouldn't be at all surprised if it was meeting Dahlman that pushed Charlie over the edge.

It's his all-or-nothing approach that bothers me the most. Either I prostitute myself completely with vaginal rejuvenation ads and underage naked pictures on the Internet, or I might as well give up. Obviously I'm learning that the marketing side of the art business (just as with any other business) requires some ideological compromises, but do I have to compromise everything? Putting aside all that post-postmodern theory I learned in college, isn't there still a fundamental difference between an artist and say a cigarette company CEO?

About five minutes into my Dahlman-induced tirade, I stop at a light and notice that there's a young blond boy in the passenger seat of a Mini Cooper who's staring at me. He has almost no chin at all and such slack facial features in general that I suspect he might have Down syndrome. I look back at him and try and nod that it's okay, I'm not crazy, but he shakes his head in response and gives me the finger.

It takes another twenty minutes of inching down Sunset to pull ahead of the Mini Cooper and stop the chinless kid from staring at me. To my surprise, it turns out that the traffic isn't caused by an accident, but by earthquake damage. On the south side of the street, one three-story building has collapsed completely and several others have the telltale jagged foundation cracks that mean they will either soon collapse or be red-tagged for demolition. And on the north side of the street, a rectangular stone chunk of an old bank façade has fallen off and crushed in the windshield of a new red Acura. The car alarm is still going off, but the pitch has worn down to a pathetic, almost whalelike whine.

By far the most bizarre sight, however, is along a strip of curb just past the bank. Tar seeps have formed shallow pools on the surface of the blacktop and trapped the shoes of several unsuspecting and now furious pedestrians. One particularly incensed elderly woman in a yellow pantsuit storms barefoot over to her El Dorado, retrieves the tire iron from the trunk, and makes a futile attempt to beat the tar back.

Another twenty minutes of traffic, and I finally reach the blinding cube of polished aluminum and Mylar-mirrored windows that constitute Dahlman's gallery.

Apparently he had it remodeled to look more Frank Gehry after the music center went up downtown, but cheaped out on the stainless steel and went with aluminum sheet siding so thin it resembles Reynolds Wrap. Back in the '70s when Dahlman used to be a music talent agent, he kept the whole brick front of his Hollywood Boulevard office plastered with giant posters of his various teen idols. The specific location was chosen due to its proximity to the Greyhound bus station and the flood of young boys and girls running away from home to "make it" in Hollywood. This, in turn, allowed him to supply music studios and casting couches throughout the city with fresh meat, and use the kickbacks to invest in hand-grooming future "stars" (mostly willowy blond boys with socks jammed down their spandex). As far as I know, Dahlman's no longer pimping out children to industry sleaze, but the one-way Mylared windows of his Melrose gallery still give me the unconscious sense that something very questionable is going on inside. Walking down the sidewalk from my car to the entrance, I see my reflection—compressed to the size of a toddler by the aftershock-warped aluminum panels—flying along on a parallel course to my own. The image is dark, twitching with rage, and contorted almost beyond recognition—a malevolent black shadow that, to my relief, waits hovering outside as I pass through the glass double doors.

Compared with the blazing aluminum along the sidewalk, the interior of the gallery is more modestly illuminated with track lighting, and it takes a little while for my eyes to adjust enough to make out my artwork lining the walls and cluttering the floor as it's being organized for the show. There's no one behind the oversized '80s chrome and glass desk, and by the time I navigate my way up to it, my pupils have dilated enough to see that the whole gallery is in fact uninhabited. I'm about to call out, when someone beats me to it.

"Just a second, Isabel." The voice comes from the open door to a back room, and is soon followed by the appearance of a slightly hawk-faced woman with short-cropped gray hair. She's wearing drawstring desert camouflage shorts that are at least a decade too young for her, and has a futuristic-looking artificial leg made out of metal tubing that starts just below her left hip. The woman has been working at the gallery ever since I first met Dahlman three months ago, and I'm almost positive her first name is Peg, but not quite positive enough to risk using it on a one-legged woman.

"How'd you know it was me?"

"I spotted you on the security camera." She smiles. "I hear congratulations are in order?"

"Congratulations?"

"No need for faux modesty around here." Peg winks.

"You heard about the *Sunday Calendar* cover?"

"The what?" I can tell by her face that she obviously has no idea what I'm talking about.

"The . . ." It suddenly occurs to me that telling her I made the cover might come off as bragging. ". . . Never mind. So why the congratulations?"

"For your boyfriend, Javier. He made *Celeb* magazine's '75 Most Luscious People' list."

"He what?"

"Gossip." Peg shakes her head. "It's awful, isn't it? Shucks open your life like an oyster and tosses the pearl into the slop bucket of public opinion."

"Wait . . . so does that mean it's not true?" I struggle with the metaphor.

"No, it's true. I was just pointing out how awful it is that people are gossiping about it. I mean, it's not as if he's the first chef to ever make the list."

She roots around under the counter, and comes up with a copy of *Celeb*. It's dog-eared to the page with Javier. Under the words "Celebrity Chef à la Mode," Javier is lounging bare-chested poolside with a bikini-clad (or at least a bikini by Brazilian standards) Mirabel Matamoros on his lap. He's feeding her strawberries dipped in chocolate from an antique silver chafing dish, and is flashing a smile that could seduce a nun. The caption reads: "If he were our chef, we'd let him do more than cook!" Considering that Mirabel is only sixteen, the picture crosses the line from scandalously smoldering to downright skeezy.

I suddenly feel an odd lightness in my legs. Not a feeling like I'm about to collapse, but conversely that I'm going to float up to the ceiling like a weather balloon. Instinctively, I grab on to the counter in an effort to stop my ascent.

"You feeling okay?" Peg reaches out and puts a hand on my forearm.

"Yeah, I'm fine. It's just ..."

"He didn't tell you he made the list?"

I shake my head. It's only been two weeks since we last talked ... three at the most. The editors at *Celeb* must have decided on the "Luscious List" months ago. They had a fucking *photo shoot*, for Christ's sake....

"Maybe he was going to surprise you."

"But the magazine's already out."

"Oh." Peg nods for a little too long, then tries her best to discreetly put the magazine away.

Despite my efforts, I continue to stare blankly at Peg while my overloaded brain attempts to recover.

"You sure you're okay?" Peg asks again.

"Yeah ... yeah, I'm fine," I lie.

"So what can I do you for?"

"I . . . Dahlman wants me to sign some contract."

"Oh right, the power of attorney thing? It's in the back, just let me get it." A miniature shock absorber device in her artificial leg makes a faint hissing noise with each step as she heads into the office.

Once she's gone, I can't help myself and reach behind the desk to grab the copy of *Celeb* again. I turn to the dog-eared page, but this time notice not just the photo of Javier, but the ad on the opposite page. It features a Jessica Simpson look-alike wearing a white wedding dress and climbing into a limo with tin cans tied to the back. With the groom waiting inside, she turns back to give a secretive (but exceptionally lewd) wink. The tag line reads: "**MAKE EVERY WEDDING WHITE!**" Underneath is the familiar "Have you talked to your doctor about VR?*" but this time with an asterisk and the footnote "*Ask about hymenoplasty!"

"Here it is." Peg returns and drops what must be a two-inch-thick contract on the desk.

"You know what." I close the magazine and drop it back on the desk next to the contract. "I'm already late for something. Maybe I should come back and sign it another time."

"But it's right here." Peg points to the contract quizzically.

"Actually, I'm sort of having second thoughts."

"Well, Dahlman's not going to like that."

"No . . . I suppose he won't."

5

Back in the Nova and driving again, the odd sensation of lightness in my legs quickly metastasizes into a borderline panic attack. My stomach clenches around the remains of the porterhouse, and my vision tunnels until just the pickup truck directly in front of me is visible. Only the two-mile–an-hour crawl of traffic along Wilshire keeps me from having an accident, while I keep going over and over the meaning of the *Celeb* photo in a fruitless attempt to come up with some innocuous explanation.

Obviously it's possible that Javier is innocent and the photo is the creation of the Mirabel Matamoros media team, but it's equally obvious that Mirabel and her media team know exactly what a photo like that implies. About all I can take heart in is the thought that since she's on a nine-hundred-calorie-a-day diet in preparation for her South America tour, she probably wasn't allowed to actually eat the chocolate-dipped strawberries.

Of course, in retrospect, Javier's apparent infidelity shouldn't come as a total surprise. When I first met him back at UC Santa Cruz, he was a militant environmentalist from Vermont who had studied the culinary arts as part of his master plan to convince people that a vegan diet didn't have to be dull. Since I wasn't a vegan (or even a vegetarian) myself, it was his unshakable conviction that attracted me—not to mention the fact that he's borderline Johnny Depp handsome—more than his actual cause. But within six months of graduating and moving down to LA, he became a personal chef to the stars, serving up endangered beluga caviar and slabs of medium-rare veal. It's not just that he turned his back so completely on the textured vegetable protein of yore (as well as just about everything else that he at least professed to believe in), but that he did it so quickly, without the least bit of remorse. And it wasn't for the money, either (his parents are New England blue bloods). As far as I can tell, he simply couldn't resist the temptation to buy in.

Jesus Christ, a sixteen-year-old wannabe Aguilera, *Javier? Are you fucking kidding me?*

Because of traffic, the drive home takes almost an hour, giving me the chance to at least partially recover. When I finally pull onto South Orange Grove Avenue, my peripheral vision has widened enough to make out an array of haphazardly parked fire trucks and emergency response vehicles clogging the rest of the street and blocking access to my apartment building. It's only when I actually get out of the Nova and approach the yellow caution tape stretched across the road that I spot the men in yellow-hooded Hazmat suits with oxygen tanks on their backs.

"What's up? Another meth lab?" I call out to a throng of

bystanders who all happen to be standing inside the caution tape.

"No es la meth. Es el pinche alquitrán." An elderly Mexican man turns around to explain.

Of course, having made the pretentious choice to study French instead of Spanish in high school, I have no idea what he means. Of the thirty or so cops and firefighters standing around, no one is actually guarding the caution tape, so I duck under it and start heading for my building. An enormous hook-and-ladder fire truck blocks my view until I'm directly across the street and can see what's wrong.

The entire pink stucco nightmare of the San Maximón Arms is listing at least twenty degrees to the left. It's as if Godzilla sat down on the roof and squished the whole north side of the building down seven or eight feet into the earth. The once visible concrete foundation is completely submerged, and several of the ground-floor apartments are on the verge themselves of becoming subterranean, with the crabgrass lawn creeping above window level. The stench of methane is overwhelming, even from twenty yards away.

"Isabel!" Chris calls to me from where he's standing with a group of firefighters, and then comes over.

"What the hell happened?" I ask.

"The building leaned."

"But . . . how?"

"The tar seepage created some kind of a giant sinkhole. They're calling in another structural engineer for a second opinion, but word is they're going to red-tag it for sure. The fire captain won't even let people get their stuff out." He shakes his head.

"What about Jello?" The thought of my cat being trapped in a collapsing building quickly beats out any worries about my paintings or other belongings. With my apartment several feet closer to the ground than usual, I can actually see her perched in the kitchen window.

"You need Jell-O?" Chris looks confused.

"My cat."

"Oh ... You better talk to the captain." He points to a man in a white fire helmet standing with two police officers in front of the building, and then follows me as I walk over.

One of the police officers—young with severe acne scars enhancing his cable TV tough-cop look—has a stun gun in his hand and is making obscene gestures with it as the apparent punch line to a joke. When they notice me, all three of them start laughing harder.

"You didn't hear that, did you?" the fire captain asks.

"Uh, no."

"So what can I do you for, then?"

"I really need to get into my apartment."

"Sorry. The building could collapse at any moment. Not to mention the potential toxicity of those fumes."

"But my cat's in there."

"I assure you, your cat will be fine." His face loses all animation and locks into a half-smile as he says this.

"In a collapsing building filled with toxic fumes?"

"Again, I'm sorry, but until the chief structural engineer gets here, no one's going in." He puts his hands on his hips in an oddly feminine gesture of determination. "And I'm going to have to ask both of you to stay behind the yellow tape."

Still in shock, I follow Chris back under the yellow tape, only to be accosted by a blonde TV reporter with eyes slightly too close together.

"Excuse me!" She shoves my Trinidadian neighbor with the

Shetland sheepdog out of the way. "Were you just rescued from this building?"

"No."

An Asian cameraman at the far end of the yellow tape breaks off from shooting establishing shots and comes over. Not wanting anything to do with TV after his disastrous child star days on *Karate*, Chris melts discreetly into the crowd.

"Were you in the building when it started to collapse?"

"No."

"Well, would you be willing to tell your story anyway?"

You gotta hand it to her—she takes her local news seriously.

"No." I shake my head.

"No?"

"No."

"How about if I were to sweeten the pot a little?" She pulls a billfold out of a hidden pocket in her miniskirt and tries to hand me a hundred-dollar bill.

"You're *paying* me to be interviewed?"

"The producers want to punch up the ratings with better-looking victims for the interviews. If your story's good enough to get me a lead, I'll double that."

Before I can answer, my cell phone starts screaming "Ride of the Valkyries" again.

"Sorry, I have to take this." I flee into the crowd and answer the phone without looking at the number.

"*Congratulations!*" Javier yells in his recently adopted Malibu surfer accent.

"Huh?" I start back towards my car.

"*The* Sunday Calendar *cover! Mirabel's stylist told me. We should celebrate!*"

"Listen, Javier, I'm having kind of a crisis here. My apartment collapsed into a giant tar sinkhole. Can I stay at your place tonight?" I decide to put any argument over *Celeb* magazine on hold for now.

"*What?*" He's obviously doing something else in the background.

"Can I stay at your apartment?" I grit my teeth and repeat myself.

"*Oh … Sorry, I sublet it. I thought I told you? Mirabel needs me staying here full-time. She's got me cooking mini sage and Manchego tortillas for her friends all hours of the night. It just didn't make sense, you know, paying for a place I never see.*"

"So you're living with her?" I try to keep any judgment out of my voice, but it's not easy. *She's fucking sixteen years old.*

"*In one of the guesthouses.*"

One of the guesthouses?

"So then … can I stay with you there?"

"*Uh …*" I can hear the momentary muffling of a hand on the receiver. "*No, I don't think that's going to work. I'm really busy cooking for the—*"

"Please?"

"*Why don't you stay with your parents?*" I hear the muffled sound again, followed by a laugh.

"Javier?"

"*Oh fuck … the roux is burning…. Gotta go. Love you.*" He hangs up.

I sit parked in the Nova with the windows rolled, swearing at the top of my lungs and pummeling the cracked vinyl dashboard with my fists for a full ten minutes, before finally calling my parents.

An hour later, I've finally managed to explain to my pathologically chatty mother that I'm coming over to stay, and am driving through downtown Hollywood. I make a left off Franklin and drift into the three-dimensional labyrinth that the streets make as they break their grid to writhe over the Hollywood Hills. This is the neighborhood I grew up in, and the sidewalks are the same ones I walked to and from elementary school on. Every lawn, every house, every palm tree seems ready to ignite with vivid childhood memories—but then for some reason doesn't. The failed landscape sputters its way back into history, vanishing in the rearview mirror.

I take another left and start up one of the tortuous roads rising from the canyon floor. Built in the '20s before the arrival of mechanical graders and housing developments, the asphalt seems less a route for automobiles than a whimsical game trail for mule deer. The road was already narrow back when fuel efficiency and compact cars were the rage, but now, with every other parked car being a behemoth Suburban or Hummer, driving it feels more like an aboveground spelunking expedition. Only a lifetime familiarity with each twist and hairpin turn of the road allows me to progress at more than a crawl. Even so, I have to shift into reverse and back up the Nova twice in order to let cars coming downhill pass.

My parents' house is the second to last on a ridge adjacent to Griffith Park and directly under the Hollywood sign. The third-to-last house is a flat-roofed ranch monstrosity with seashell-inlaid lima green stucco walls. It was originally built and is still occupied by Armando Chevre, a fitness celebrity of national renown during the '30s who once towed a red car trolley all the way from Santa Monica to downtown with his teeth. He's now well into his nineties and still insists on displaying both his physical prowess and his remarkably carcinoma-free tan every time I see him.

The last house is a Disneyesque miniature castle that dates back to the silent film days and for the last twenty-five or so years has been occupied by a former '70s porn star who has since gained respectability as a New Age motivational speaker. Despite her checkered past, my parents taught me as a toddler to refer to her as Aunt Vanessa, and have always behaved quite neighborly towards her—even when she ceremoniously presented me with a copy of *The Joy of Sex* and a pocket vibrator on my eleventh birthday.

My parents' home is one of the four stilt houses built along the ridge. The hillside tumbles straight down at a sixty-degree grade, but the single-story house is propped up on two tubular steel supports that anchor in a V some fifty feet below, allowing the bulk of the structure to float with apparent precariousness in thin air. According to the earthquake retrofitters my mother called in after the Northridge quake, however, the steel beams are sunk deep into granite bedrock, and the house is (at least in theory) safer than most—a fact that's only marginally reassuring when the floor sways six or seven inches in either direction for ten minutes after every aftershock.

As I pull up and park behind my father's Vespa scooter, I spot my mother's hair—a bright red lion's mane that stands out like a fire truck—down in the treacherously terraced garden with Armando. They both come up the redwood steps to greet me.

"My God, honey! You're thin as a bird!" My mother shifts a basket of heirloom vegetables to her other hand so she can give me a hug.

"Mom, you can eat like a bird, but I don't think birds are particularly thin."

"You should drink organic whey with raw buckwheat honey. At least a quart a day," Armando advises, shaking my hand with a bone-crunching grip. He gave up what little modesty he possessed back in his eighties, and as if to emphasize this point, he does a one-handed push-up off the curb.

"Sweetie, I put out new toothpaste and dental floss in the guest bathroom. Just in case it takes a few days for them to fix your apartment." My mother nods excitedly.

"Mom, my apartment sank into the tar. They're not going to fix it."

"That's horrible, honey!" She shakes her head. "But you know, it's probably for the best."

"The best?"

"With your income, you should buy a house. Renting is just pissing your money away."

"You really have lost weight!" Armando makes an entirely inappropriate two-handed grab at my waist. "You have to keep your strength up if you want to live to a hundred." He demonstrates by doing another one-handed push-up off the curb with the other arm, and then offers me a Japanese eggplant out of my mother's vegetable basket.

"I think I'll fix myself something inside." I force a half-smile and start heading for the door.

"Where's that chisel-jawed boyfriend of yours?" my mother calls after me.

"I told you on the phone, he's having an affair with the Latina Britney Spears."

"Oh . . . I thought you were just being pessimistic."

There really is no appropriate response to this, so I simply grind my molars.

"I had quite a number of affairs in my youth," Armando proclaims, as he starts doing a series of curious bending exercises. "Of course, that was before genital warts became such a problem."

My mother used to be a chain-smoking children's book author, but when she quit smoking to get pregnant with me, she discovered that (at least for her) typing and tobacco were inextricably linked, and was forced to give it up. Relentlessly cheerful and buoyed on a bottomless sea of '50s-style denial (despite being a former hippie), she went into commercial real estate and made a killing selling downtown high-rises to the Japanese during the 1980s.

The children's books were all about a group of junior high students who transform a Bluebird school bus into a fusion-powered spacecraft and begin to secretly colonize the moon. For some unexplained reason, I was strictly forbidden to read them, and in order to insure this, my mother kept only foreign-language editions around the house. When I finally discovered the entire series in its native English buried in a friend's bookshelf during a slumber party, I hid from the other girls in a guest bathroom and read them all through in one night. With the exception of my mother's curious habit of using a conjugation of the word "insinuate" in almost every paragraph, nothing about the books stood out as even remotely unusual, and I failed to discover why she didn't want me to read them.

Once in the house, I head straight for the computer in the den and check my Web site. Since my parents don't have a censorship program running, it comes right up with the naked photos of me on the *home page* no less. Toby was actually a pretty talented photographer for a nineteen-year-old, so the pictures themselves aren't really that bad, but then having naked photos of myself on the Internet is humiliating enough.

I'm about to close the browser when a Flash pop-up ad appears. It shows a disheveled girl stumbling out of a college frat house in the early-morning light. Half-naked frat boys are leaning out of all the windows of the house cheering her as she leaves. The main text reads "LIKE IT NEVER HAPPENED!" and across the bottom is the now familiar "Have you talked to your doctor about VR?"

Dahlman, you are one sick bastard.

I close the browser and shut down the whole computer for good measure, then head to the kitchen. In stark contrast to my own minimalist tendencies when it comes to food storage, my mother believes wholeheartedly in the psychological benefits of keeping a bountiful larder. With four different cranberry juice blends and at least thirteen kinds of raw milk cheese, there's more food in the fridge and surrounding cupboards than in the average strip mall minimart. I pull out six jumbo-sized brown eggs, three of the cheeses, butter, and a Ziploc bag of shiitake mushrooms. Somehow the massive porterhouse only seems to have increased my appetite.

My parents recently installed an absurdly powerful 20,000-BTU nine-burner restaurant stove, and it takes me a few minutes to figure out how to lower the gas below flame-thrower, but eventually I discover a simmer setting that seems to work. Using an equally absurd fourteen-inch copper skillet, I start to work on what I estimate to be a two-thousand-calorie omelet. It's only when I finish and fix a cranberry and soda that I glance through the window and notice my father sitting on the back porch with a pair of binoculars.

He's a small man (I'm guessing 135 pounds), with camel blond hair and a round face. Back in the '70s, he was a physicist at Cal Tech when he started studying the effect of dark matter on the elliptical orbit of planets. All was well and good—there was even talk of his being short-listed for the Nobel Prize—until the day he typed all the available planet orbit information for our solar system into one of those old-fashioned room-sized computers. It took a couple days for all the computations to finish, but when it did, my father had made the discovery of a lifetime: the "Pinball Theory of Apocalypse." Apparently (and I have never understood the math behind this) the planets in our solar system are gradually losing their stable orbits, and will begin colliding into one another on October 9, 2049. Of course, everyone initially took him to be a crackpot, but when he published in *Science* and physicists around the world began to crunch the numbers themselves, it became clear that far from being a crackpot, he actually was the true prophet of the apocalypse.

And then a strange thing happened. People began ignoring him. Journals refused to publish his articles, physicists failed to return his phone calls, and students stopped taking his classes. Apparently nobody, not even hard-core scientists, want to be confronted with the end of the world. He eventually resigned his tenured position and, since my mother was raking in more money than they could ever need from her real estate deals, became more or less a hermit. But at least once a year, some young grad student will show up at the house with a stack of papers and a laptop eager to prove him wrong—only to leave sobbing uncontrollably.

Taking my colossal omelet and cranberry juice with me, I head out onto the porch, careful to stay clear of the rail and its hundred-foot vertiginous drop.

"Mom says your apartment's a goner." He puts down his binoculars and takes a hit off the joint in the ashtray next to him. For a man convinced the world is ending, he has an apparently congenital lack of anxiety. Not once in my twenty-six years have I seen him flinch.

"How'd you know that?" I ask, realizing there's no way my mother could have gotten to the back porch without first passing through the den and kitchen.

He holds up his cell phone in explanation, then offers me a hit off his joint.

"No thanks ... What's with the binoculars?"

"They're out there digging a break and lighting backfires to try and keep the neighborhood from going up like Silverlake and Los Feliz." He points to a distant line of firefighters working up near the "Hollywood" sign in Griffith Park.

"Is the fire headed this way?"

"Yep." He points to the red emergency water drop helicopters that are hovering to the east over by Mount Hollywood. "Shouldn't reach here unless the Santa Ana winds pick up."

"Are the Santa Anas supposed to pick up?"

"Yep." He takes another toke.

I join him on an adjacent chaise lounge and eat my omelet quietly for a while, hoping for some of his antianxiety to rub off on me, but it doesn't.

"Dad, I ..." It's been at least ten years since I've tried to talk frankly with him. "I'm having some trouble."

"Is this about Javier porking that sixteen-year-old?"

"How'd you know about that?"

"Mom." He holds up his cell phone again. "If you need an untraceable handgun, that psychiatrist who lives down on Chula Loma has a whole drawerful. He takes them off suicidal patients."

"A handgun?" As usual, this isn't turning out to be the run-of-the-mill father-daughter chat. But then again, my current predicament isn't particularly "run of the mill" either. "No ... but thanks. Javier's really not worth it."

"So what's the problem? Your subterranean apartment?"

"Sort of ... Actually, no. It's ... Dad, do you think I'm a sellout?"

He pinches out his joint and ponders this for a moment.

"Is there really still such a thing as 'selling out'? I thought all that don't-trust-anyone-over-thirty stuff went out with the Grizzly Adams beard and crappy homemade Joe Cocker tie-dyes."

"Well, okay, then how about just for argument's sake?"

"Do you want a devil's advocate or an impartial observer?"

"Let's go with the observer."

"Okay, then in my admittedly layman's opinion, I'd say your

paintings are not only good, but an honest expression of how you see the world. Therefore, no, I don't think you're a sellout."

"But what about the rest of it? I mean, Dahlman's trying to get me to do vaginal rejuvenation ads and turn my life into a Lindsay Lohan movie and . . ." I decide to leave out the part about the underage naked photos.

"I see." He stares off at the fire helicopters as he thinks about it. "Well, I guess it comes down to two questions. First, do *you* still think there's such a thing as 'selling out'? And second, if 'selling out' is still a viable concept in the new millennium, then do *you* think that having naked photos of yourself all over the Internet is selling out?"

"You saw the photos?"

"Your mother told me."

"Sorry."

"So then, what's your answer?"

"To what?"

"Question number two."

This loop in logic throws me, and I fall silent. As is his custom, my father doesn't follow up. I try to finish my omelet, but my appetite seems to have vanished again. I'm about to head back into the kitchen, when his cell phone rings.

"Yep . . . yep . . . nope . . . yep." He hangs up and turns to me. "Mom says she's called you twice, but your cell keeps going to voice mail. It must be the crappy reception."

I pull out my phone, check to make sure it's on, and head back into the kitchen to rinse my plate and glass. While my father may have failed to calm me, the hundred or so grams of fat in the omelet at least make me sluggish. Before I can even get the dish into the dishwasher, my cell phone starts screaming Wagner again.

"Hi, Mom," I answer without looking at the screen.

"*What?*" Javier is thrown by my greeting.

"Sorry, I thought . . ."

"*Look, you're right, we need to talk.*"

"I didn't say we needed to talk. I said I needed a place to stay."

"*I think it's best if we did this in person. Can you come over now?*"

"I'm already at my parents'." I glance at the stove clock to confirm that it's rush hour.

"*I don't want to fight over the phone.*" Javier finally drops the phony Malibu accent. *Shit. He really is fucking her.*

"So you're asking me to drive all the way out to Bel Air so we can fight in person? Because I'll tell you, an hour and a half in bumper-to-bumper traffic is just what—"

"*Isabel, don't make this any harder than it already is.*"

"Actually, you're the one that's making it harder."

"*Please?*"

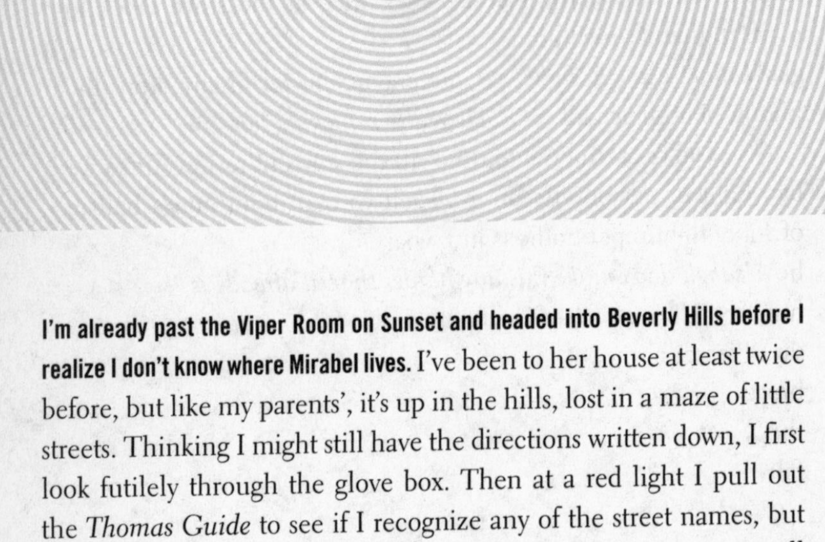

7

I'm already past the Viper Room on Sunset and headed into Beverly Hills before I realize I don't know where Mirabel lives. I've been to her house at least twice before, but like my parents', it's up in the hills, lost in a maze of little streets. Thinking I might still have the directions written down, I first look futilely through the glove box. Then at a red light I pull out the *Thomas Guide* to see if I recognize any of the street names, but of course I don't. As a last-ditch effort, I try to call Javier on my cell phone, only to have it go straight to voice mail. It's taken almost an hour to drive out here, and now I'm not going to be able to find it.

This thought vanishes when I look up and suddenly have to stomp on the brake to keep from plowing into a teenage boy in the middle of the street straddling the dotted yellow line between the right and left lanes. The Nova skids a few feet but, miracle car that it is, stops just in time.

The boy is Latino, wearing filthy khakis and a see-through wife-beater undershirt. He has a can of spray paint in one hand and a brown paper bag in the other, and looks almost as skinny as me, but with an oversized head balanced precariously on his swizzle-stick neck. The cars behind me begin hitting their horns, and with each honk, the boy starts shuffling his feet and turning slowly in a circle just short of 360 degrees.

"Hey!" I lean out the window and yell, not knowing what else to say.

The boy shuffles 180 degrees to look at me. His eyes have a glazed waste look that matches his fixed meaningless smile.

"You can't just stand there," I say, stating the obvious.

The boy tries to spray more paint into the paper bag, but misses by a few inches and manages instead to produce a large splotch of Day-Glo yellow on his forearm. After a moment's confusion, he drops the spray can and begins trying to inhale the paint fumes directly off his skin. Before I can think of anything else to say, a vintage BMW pulls around me and squeezes past the boy, brushing ever so slightly against his arm. Despite the gentleness of the impact, the boy bounces violently off the side of the car and falls face-first into the asphalt.

The woman in the BMW speeds away, and I get out of the Nova to help the boy up.

"*Orale* … what's up?" The boy squints in my general direction.

"You're in the middle of the street."

"Yeah?" he answers with no discernible emotion.

"You can't just stand in the street. You'll get hit by a car."

"You know…." He takes another hit off his forearm. "… sometimes, some days … you just get hit by cars."

I walk him over to a lawn chair and a sign for "Maps to Stars'

Homes" set up on the curb, then pull the Nova over so cars can get past. When I return to the boy, he's dumped out a grocery bag full of cheaply printed maps to get to another can of spray paint.

"That stuff is going to kill you," I point out.

"You know what your problem is, man? Carpe diem. You need to seize the day."

"Seize the day?" I don't know why this particular phrase strikes me as so offensive, but it does. "Look, kid, instead of just huffing paint until my brain returns to a primordial state of ooze, I actually put it on canvas. If dedicating your life to the arts isn't 'seizing the day,' I don't know what is."

"It's not."

"No?"

"It's pure escapism." He sprays more paint into the grocery bag and takes another hit.

Realizing the futility of arguing with a boy whose brain is rapidly dissolving in paint thinner, I'm about to walk back to the Nova when I again notice the "Maps to Stars' Homes" that he's dumped out on the sidewalk.

"Does that map have Mirabel Matamoros's house on it?"

"No." He shakes his head. "She only bought that house like six months ago."

"Do you know where it is?"

"Twenty dollars and I'll show you on the map."

"How about ten?"

"Twenty."

"You do realize that I just saved your life?"

"Life is cheap. Twenty."

It seems a little pricey for an address that's less than a mile away, but it appears to be my last option.

"Give me your *Thomas Guide*." He takes the twenty and holds out his hand.

"Aren't you going to use one of your maps?"

"These *pinche* maps suck."

I hand him the *Thomas Guide* from my car, and (despite his solvent-saturated brain) he flips to the right page without even looking in the index, then sprays a small blob of Day-Glo paint where her house is.

"It has concertina wire on top of a green wrought-iron entrance gate." He hands the map back. "You can't miss it."

"I've been there before, I just forgot the address." I feel the asinine need to show that I'm not a starstruck Midwestern tourist.

"Whatever." The kid shrugs and pulls away from me, stumbling into the street again—a limp mannequin suspended by vapors. One of the cars down the street honks, and he begins his almost-360-degree turn again.

8

Using the map, I find the house no problem, but there isn't any parking allowed on the street, so I have to buzz at the gate. Instead of receiving an answer over the intercom, I'm greeted in person by the single largest man I have ever seen in my life. The guy could dwarf Shaq. He has one of those Secret Service–style IFB earplugs, and has apparently either replaced or been added to Mirabel's previous enormous bodyguard.

"This is a private residence. I'm going to have to ask you to leave." Despite his size, he has a high-pitched Mike Tyson voice. He takes a step towards the car, and I involuntarily drop into a defensive cringe.

"It's okay, I'm Javier's girlfriend. He invited me over."

"Javier's girlfriend? You mean the chef?" He laughs. "Haven't heard that one before."

"I'm serious."

"What? Did you get that from *Celeb*? You stalkarazzi need to do your research. Javier doesn't have a girlfriend."

"Yes he does," I answer stupidly. "Can't you just tell him I'm here?"

"No."

"Please?"

He cold-stares me for a minute, but I manage not to look away, and he finally calls somebody on his walkie-talkie.

"There, I called it in, okay? You happy? Now it's time for you to leave. . . ." Suddenly his hand goes to his ear as he listens to something coming over his IFB earplug. His expression changes to one of bewilderment, and he lets go of the earplug. "Sorry about that. Are you Isabel?"

"That's what I've been trying to tell you." I do my best to sound pissed off, but with his seven-foot-plus bulk hanging over me, it comes out more as though I'm pleading.

"Can I see your driver's license?"

I pull out the silver cigarette case I use as a wallet and show it to him.

"Again, sorry about that. Follow me."

He opens the electronic gate and leads the Nova with six-foot strides up the crushed-gravel drive to a flat parking area in front of a house-sized garage. Both the garage and the house itself are built in a jarring combination of Rustic Provence and Greek Revival (i.e., faux Corinthian columns sponge-painted an earthy yellow and then heated to a cracked patina). I'd pity any future archaeologist trying to decipher such a mess, except that—at least according to my father's "Pinball Apocalypse" theory—there won't be any future archaeologists. Javier told me it was built by a former Iranian caviar mogul whose wife stabbed him in the thigh with a barbecue fork during an argument. The wound was relatively minor, but unfortunately for the former caviar mogul (and his wife, who's now in prison), the raw chicken juice on the barbecue fork got into his bloodstream and he died of septicemia a week later. At just over twenty-three thousand square feet, the house provides exactly the sort of cozy nest a 110-pound emancipated sixteen-year-old pop star needs.

The enormous bodyguard leads me through a series of rooms decorated to the hilt in conflicting styles that seem to have been chosen at random—a Santa Fe/Hawaiian luau entrance hall (complete with tiki torches), an English country sitting room with postmodern corrugated cardboard furniture, and a Louis XIV dining room with glazed concrete flooring and enough mirrors lining the walls to give Versailles a run for its money. We finally come out onto a natural flagstone terrace and an enormous artificial black lava rock pool with waterfalls and a Playboy Mansion–style grotto. The top of the lava rock blends (or more accurately, fails to blend) with the real thirty-foot cliff left over from when they excavated into the hillside for the pool. But this "real" cliff is probably the oddest sight of all, because despite the eighty-plus-degree weather, it's covered in snow.

"Please wait here." The bodyguard turns and walks back inside.

I stand gawking at the artificial snow and don't respond. The other enormous bodyguard, who I met previously, is filling in bald patches in the snow with a giant movie studio blower device, while Mirabel (wearing only her sub-Brazilian bikini) is roped in and climbing the cliff with what looks like the help of two authentic Sherpas (one on belay, the other instructing from directly below her). As if this scene isn't disturbing enough, Mirabel has both legs wide open, with her right foot wedged in a particularly high foothold, and is consequently thrusting the crotch of her thong bikini into the face of the instructor Sherpa as she tries to step up. All three of the men are so actively trying to avoid looking at this that they notice my entrance immediately and give embarrassed nods.

The terrace has a small bar set up on one side, but nowhere to sit. Feeling like a little pick-me-up might be just what I need to overcome my shock (not to mention help me through what's bound to be an awkward conversation with Javier), I head over to check out the bar, but the only thing behind it are cases of electrolyte-enhanced bottled water. I'm not exactly sure what electrolytes are, so I decide to leave them be and go back to watching Mirabel climb.

The first time I met her (actually, the only time), she was meeting with her label to decide what stylistic approach to take with her new album. They had three different full-sized posters of her on the thirty-foot dining room table: one of her as a Paris fashion runway interpretation of a punk rocker (complete with a pink Swarovski crystal anarchy symbol hand-beaded on her combat jacket), one of her as good girl/virgin (dressed chastely in a white turtleneck with a honking big crucifix around her neck), and the last as a straightforward slut (straddling a stripper pole in—surprise surprise—a minuscule bikini). In support of each look, they also had prerecorded music samples of bubblegum punk rock, bubblegum good girl/virgin, and bubblegum slut. Mirabel came off at the meeting like the CEO of a Fortune 500 company, discussing in depth the ramifications of each look with the three middle-aged label reps. Despite her total lack of talent, I could almost respect her for the guts and drive it took to turn herself into a pop phenomenon, but the Swarovski crystal anarchy symbol was really unforgivable.

A few minutes later, Javier (dressed professionally in his whites and chef hat) appears at the door with two steaming bowls of what looks like stew. Instead of nodding, he gives me a blank look, and then climbs the grotto stairs up to the cliff and hands the bowls to the Sherpas before coming over.

"Hey, Isabel," he says casually, as if it hasn't been two weeks since I've seen him.

"Javier, why is Mirabel climbing an artificially frozen cliff with the help of two Sherpas?"

"Huh? Oh, they're helping her train for her part in the remake of *The Eiger Sanction*. She doesn't do any climbing in the movie, but, you know, she wants to learn for veracity's sake."

"Veracity? Isn't the Eiger in Switzerland, not Nepal?"

"Yeah, but these guys are the best. They've worked on Everest expeditions."

"Oh."

There's a pause as we both try and come up with something to say. But since Javier is now watching Mirabel's climb, the pause gets uncomfortable. I notice that the Sherpas have abandoned Mirabel's belay rope entirely to eat the stew (Javier's cooking can have that effect on you). For some reason, I keep thinking about the Day-Glo-paint-sniffing boy in the street and his advice to "carpe diem." Not only is Javier downright gorgeous, but he's by far the best lay I've ever had. It suddenly occurs to me that once he gets up the courage to dump me, we'll never have sex again. I'm not generally such an abject horn-dog, but with all the stress I've been under in the last few months, the idea of a grand finale roll in the hay sounds surprisingly tempting.

"Do you wanna have sex?" I startle even myself by asking.

"Now?" Javier breaks off from watching Mirabel and focuses on me with his wolf blue eyes and oddly blank face.

"Come on, it'll be fun."

"Isabel, I'm working." He points to his chef's hat to emphasize the point.

"I know, but ... it could just be a kitchen table quickie."

"That's romantic."

One of the Sherpas calls out to Javier in what I suppose is Nepalese. Javier smiles and answers back in what surprisingly also sounds like fluent Nepalese.

"You speak Nepalese?" I ask him.

"That's beside the point." Javier kisses me on the forehead in a gesture that is right on the line between cute and patronizing. It's that schizo former vegan/current veal-eater personality of his again. I'm not even sure *he* knows which of his myriad loving gestures are heartfelt and which are pure Machiavellian manipulation. Looking up into his blank face, I get no clue. In fact, his face is entirely without expression ... not to mention wrinkles or crow's-feet.

"Javier, did you ... did you get Botox?"

"No."

"You did! You're not even thirty—why the hell are you getting Botox?"

"It's complicated, okay?" I think he's trying to look serious, but it's hard to tell.

"Is this what you dragged me out here to talk about? Your 'complicated' decision to get Botox?" If he's going to dump me, there's no reason I should make it easy for him.

"No ... It's a long story." Even without the facial expressions, I can tell he's nervous by the way his eyes keep glancing up at Mirabel on the cliff. "Look, I haven't finished dinner prep, but if you hang out for like an hour, we can talk."

"I have to go to a party at some guy named Alex Tzu's house."

"*The* Alex Tzu?"

"You know who he is?"

"Yeah, he's one of those tech-boom billionaire philanthropists. He's practically as rich as Bill Gates . . . well, maybe half as rich."

"Really? He's been buying my paintings."

"*Your* paintings?" Despite the Botox, Javier manages to raise an eyebrow in surprise.

"Fuck you."

As if in response, the bodyguard running the artificial snow machine changes angles and accidentally blows 110-pound Mirabel clear off the cliff. The fall is less than ten feet, but she lands on the jagged fake lava rock and scrapes down several yards before coming to a stop. Considering she's wearing only a bikini (and not much of that), it makes me wince, despite the fact that I hate her. To my surprise, Javier doesn't run over, but stands with me, staring at the accident like a rubbernecker.

"Is she okay?" I ask.

"It looked kind of bad." Javier shakes his head.

"Well?"

"Well what?"

"Aren't you going to try and help her?"

"She doesn't like other people's help. She's independent that way."

"Javier, are you fucking her?" It just pops out. Somehow all these aftershocks really seem to be screwing up my timing.

"Yes." He nods blankly.

"You are?" I'm not stunned by the truth, but by the fact that he'd just come out and tell me the truth.

"I thought you knew."

My admittedly histrionic attempt to storm off indignantly is seriously hampered by the free-form layout of Mirabel's mansion. Somehow I make a wrong turn and end up in a Victorian sitting room filled with vintage video arcade games and Skee-Ball machines. I then try to retrace my steps back to the pool, but end up instead in a room with a '70s orange shag rug conversation pit and glassed-in antique walnut bookshelves filled with what must be the entire series of *The Complete Idiot's Guide*. They cover everything from understanding Judaism, to building your own home, to how to crochet.

"You are not authorized to be in this room. Please leave immediately."

The voice is coming from a security camera in the far corner of the room, and is loud enough to make me jump.

"Can you hear me?" I ask the camera.

"Yes."

"Then how the hell do I get out of here?"

"Cross the conversation pit, pass through the hanging beads, and follow the sixteenth-century Portuguese-tiled hallway to the open portcullis on your right."

I can tell by his voice that I'm not the first person to get lost at Mirabel's. I trip on the shag rug descending into the conversation pit, and swear I can hear him chuckling through the camera speaker, but the directions turn out to be correct and I emerge from the hallway into the Santa Fe/Hawaiian luau entrance hall.

However, I'm not alone. Still in her bikini (and still bleeding from deep gashes on her legs and arms), the four-foot-eleven Mirabel is standing with two enormous white pit bulls. Her arms are crossed aggressively and her head is moving in a practiced

Puerto Rican tough-girl "Oh no you didn't!" turkey bob. The pit bulls are obviously there to be threatening, but the fact that they immediately trot over and start playfully nuzzling my hands negates this effect.

"He's *my* man now, bitch. You best stay away." Mirabel's Latina gangbanger accent almost passes, but there's still a little Salt Lake City flatness that her speech coach needs to work on.

"Okay." I kneel down to pet the two pit bulls briefly, then start heading for the front door.

"You think you're better than me just because you're old enough to put naked *puta* pictures of yourself on the Internet?"

"No." I feign indifference, but that one struck home.

"Is that all you got to say?"

"Pretty much." The pit bulls follow me, and I have trouble opening the door without letting them out.

"Escobar! Noriega! *¡Vengan aquí!*" she calls the dogs, and they reluctantly trot over to her. "I've seen your art, you know. The stupid paintings with stupid celebrities in them. They suck."

"Well, you're certainly entitled to your opinion." I finally get the door open.

"I don't know what Javier ever saw in a pasty old white bitch like you."

"A shared lack of personal conviction?" I suggest.

Clearly this goes over her head, and she furrows her brow. Apparently she hasn't yet followed Javier into the expressionless land of Botox, but the nose job is pretty obvious. Meanwhile Escobar and Noriega trot back over to nuzzle my hand again.

"You know I'll fight for my man," Mirabel finally attempts a counter.

"He's all yours." Since the dogs are actually wider than me, I manage to slip through the door while holding it too close for them to follow.

"You're fucking right he is!" she yells as I close the door behind me.

9

Driving through the twilit hills on my way to Alex Tzu's house, I suddenly have to slam on the brakes to avoid plowing into the tar that's seeping up everywhere onto the road. It's only after I come to a full stop and get out of the car to examine the rivulets of black asphalt that I realize they're just the normal filling for the cracks in the road.

Clearly I'm losing my mind.

As if to confirm this thought, the moment I get back behind the wheel of the Nova, I burst out sobbing like a fucking idiot. It's not like I ever seriously thought of Javier as long-term-relationship material, but I have been dating him for *six years*. Six goddamn years and he dumps me for some fucking pseudo-Latina sixteen-year-old emancipated Mormon pop star whore? Two days before my debut gallery show?

Since I'm not normally the type to be bushwhacked by hysterical crying jags, I don't have any tissues in the car, and have to blow my nose on an old Roscoe's Chicken and Waffles T-shirt I find on the backseat floor. I pull over to the side of the road and crank up the block of early-'80s pop garbage that's playing on the radio, but even the ludicrousness of bawling to Bonnie Tyler's "Total Eclipse of the Heart" fails to halt the tears.

That fucking bastard.

That fucking bastard.

That fucking bastard.

That fucking bastard ...

10

Alex Tzu's house is off of Mulholland, perched on one of the multimillion-dollar lots above the Mt. Olympus development. I follow a long and narrow driveway bordered on both sides by unkempt oleander bushes in full bloom, until I reach an odd plain of sun-grayed asphalt where several absurdly tricked-out SUVs and a lovingly restored purple Volkswagen microbus are haphazardly parked. The moment I step out of the car and into the night, I feel a wave of mild vertigo and have to lean an arm against the car roof for support. Although I'm certain that I couldn't be more than a thousand feet above sea level, the air feels thin. A rotting three-foot gray picket fence surrounds the drive to provide a feeble barrier against the empty blackness of the night beyond it.

"Where the hell have you been?" Dahlman waddles down the drive towards me, wearing his standard evening attire of black jeans and potbelly-snug black V-neck sweater.

"Sobbing uncontrollably by the side of the road," I croak, my throat still tight.

"Well, hurry the fuck up then." Dahlman is unfazed by my response. He pulls a dress out of a brown shopping bag and tosses it to me.

"What's this for?"

"It's for you. The photographer from the *LA Times* is supposed to be here."

I unfold the dress. It's a dark blue Suzie Wong–style cheongsam with black embroidery and a matching black Mandarin collar.

"You've got to be kidding. I'll look like a geisha."

"Geishas are Japanese, that's Chinese," Dahlman corrects me.

"It's too small." I hold it up to my chest.

"In case you haven't noticed, you've been shrinking a bit lately."

"You're crazy. I'm not going to wear this."

"Let me put it this way. Would you wear it for half of three hundred and fifty thousand dollars?" He pulls out the purple check and starts waving it in my face again.

"Alright alright! Where am I supposed to change?" I look around the lot.

"Just hurry it up." Dahlman glances at his watch. "We're becoming less fashionably late by the second."

I look around in vain a second time for an appropriate place to change, then walk behind the purple VW microbus. It shields me from the house, but not from whatever is beyond the fence. When I edge up to it to look over, my mild vertigo becomes severe.

Just inches beyond the fence, the parking lot's asphalt breaks off abruptly and drops into a sheer cliff. About a hundred feet below, an impenetrable layer of clouds is convecting with a faint orange luminescence. It takes me a moment to realize that the glowing clouds are being lit up by the invisible city beneath me.

"Hello? Isabel?" Dahlman calls to me from over by the car.

"Sorry." I move back behind the microbus. "Have you ever looked over the edge here?"

"I try not to."

I strip off my T-shirt and jeans, shivering more because of my recent crying jag than the cold, and slither into the dress. The general fit is actually right, but the hemline comes down to only about an inch and a half below the V of my crotch.

"There's no way in hell I'm going to wear this!" I look down at the bare white stilts of my legs.

"If tonight goes well, you can add another fifty grand to this check."

"I look like a prostitute." I walk around from behind the microbus to show him.

"Not at all." He hands me a matching purse and a pair of embroidered dark blue slippers. "More like an escort."

The house itself stands above the parking lot at the top of a short cactus-studded incline—a textured beige stucco behemoth that floats awkwardly between Bauhaus and Mission style, but with a curious Victorian tower that rises narrowly above the top story like a chimney. While it's clearly an attempt at postmodern appropriation, it seems less to synergistically juxtapose the three architectural styles than to humiliate them. All the windows are dark except for a few on the first floor that are dimly flickering red.

The only path that leads off from the asphalt lot goes not towards the house, but wraps around back along the gray picket fence until it reaches a brick stairway that climbs up to a yard.

In contrast to the orange clouds and the red first-floor windows, the glow that comes off the yard is a celestial cool blue which, as we reach the top of the brick stairs, I realize is coming from the underwater lights of a pool and adjacent Jacuzzi. There aren't any other lights, but I can make out a number of shadowy figures moving through the mist hovering over the glowing water.

"Oh, and remember," Dahlman whispers to me as we cross the lawn and approach the pool. "Don't make cracks about 9/11. He was there."

"Why on earth would I make cracks about 9/11?"

"Hey, I'm just covering all the bases. You artists do some fucked-up things."

"So which one's Alex?" It occurs to me that I have no idea what he looks like.

"The tall Welsh-Chinese guy. Always wears a black suit. Could be a hundred and twenty degrees out and that guy's in a black suit."

We reach the flagstone terrace that borders the pool, and Dahlman immediately vanishes into a crowd of teenage girls who look like they're dressed for the Oscars—including the diamond jewelry. I spin 180 degrees and stroll towards what looks like a bar on the far side of the pool. The only person actually in the pool is a tan boy of about sixteen dressed competitively in a minuscule black Speedo with matching swim cap and goggles. He's swimming perfect freestyle laps without a splash, while three topless (and possibly bottomless) underage girls in the Jacuzzi pass a joint and watch.

Raised a couple feet above pool level in the corner of the yard is a redwood deck with several green chaise lounge chairs. A crowd of teenage boys in everything from Marc Jacobs to swim trunks mill about on the deck surrounding a central face that I recognize as belonging to the teen star of a recently canceled reality TV show. He has a can of Guinness in one hand and a Cohiba cigar in the other, but is still unable to shake his towheaded look of corn-fed innocence (the look that probably got him the reality show in the first place). There's just the slightest bit of panic in his eyes, and I wonder if he has any idea that he'll probably end up like my former child actor/building superintendent Chris in another ten years.

By the time I reach the bar at the far end of the pool, I'm convinced that in addition to being a billionaire, Alex Tzu is a full-blown pedophile. Unfortunately, instead of liquor, the bar is covered with silver platters of deviled eggs (doesn't anyone serve booze at a bar anymore?). Disappointed, but somehow starving again, I'm about to try one when a bullet-headed man in kelly green trousers steps out from around the back of the deck and heads straight for me. He has a Baccarat triple old-fashioned glass in one hand and waves its dark brown contents over the silver egg platters.

"Terribly rude, isn't it?" he asks in a slightly slurred baritone while eyeballing my blatantly visible inner thighs.

"What?"

"Not having drinks outside. Instead you have to trek your way into that satanic living room and fix a drink alone. All by yourself. It's antisocial. It's punishment."

"I'm not sure I'd go that far."

"Oh. You did want a drink though, didn't you?"

He raises his arms in what I suppose is intended as a disarming gesture, but instead causes his hypertrophied trapezius muscles to form a violent triangle from ear to shoulder. His back follows suit and creates a complementary triangle of lateral dorsi that narrows brutally from his powerful shoulders to a pair of little-boy legs. Combined with his close-cropped bullet head, these features give him such an aeronautic intensity that I half expect him to leap the gray picket fence and soar like a condor over the city below.

"Uh, yes," I finally answer.

"Sorry if I seem a bit Swiss, but I've never been very good at cocktail party talk. I mean, there's not a lot of idle chitchat in my line of work. If you know what I mean."

Having no idea what he means, I stare blankly at him and hope I won't have to find out.

"Want an egg?" he asks, switching tactics.

"What?"

"A deviled egg." He scoops one off the bar with a spade-shaped hand. "They're sublime. Cordelia makes them herself. Has the paprika FedExed from Budapest."

"No thanks." I decide not to prolong the conversation by asking who Cordelia is. The spade-shaped hand hesitates, then changes directions in midair and shovels the egg into his own mouth. He swallows it in one gulp, closing his eyes, then opens them again to resume his examination of my inner thighs. "Where did you say that satanic living room was again?" I initiate escape protocol.

"Over there." He points to the flickering red windows I noticed when I first arrived. "Want me to show you?"

"No, I think I can find it myself."

He arches his eyebrows for a second, then lets them fall. Then back up again they go.

"Hey! You're that artist, aren't you?"

"Depends which one you're talking about."

"The one Cordelia's obsessed with."

"Possibly."

"Can I have your number?" He leans down to lift the leg of his kelly green trousers and pulls a graffiti-sized permanent marker out of his sock.

"I have a boyfriend." Which I realize is still at least technically true.

"I see." He holds up his spade-shaped hand, then performs a parade drill about-face and slowly walks away, a triangle of defeat.

As soon as he's gone, I grab a deviled egg off one of the platters. For the life of me, I can't taste the paprika.

The flagstone surrounding the pool ends just beyond the deviled egg bar, where a small lava rock gas fire pit and brick grill sit dormant. Beyond them, I can see another loose brick path that leads back down to the gray picket fence skirting the property, and then disappears mysteriously behind the far side of the raised redwood deck. Realizing that this is where the bullet-headed man must have come from, I'm curious to see where it goes, but don't want to take the risk of running into him again. Besides, I need a drink first.

Snagging another egg off the bar, I walk back past the pool and lawn until I reach the glass-paneled door to the house. The door is slightly ajar, so I slide it the rest of the way open and step into a large unoccupied room. Paintings cover all the wall space between the windows, with the exception of one corner where a curiously placed L-shaped bar juts out. The whole zinc surface of the bar is cluttered with liquor bottles, and built into the angle of the L-shaped base is a flat-screen TV. The sound has been muted, but the pictures run with continuous shots of the brushfire raging through Silverlake.

It takes a moment to realize both that these are the same televised fires that were flickering red in the windows when I first arrived, and that all the paintings on the wall are mine.

"You like them?"

"Huh?" I spin around to see a tall, thin, possibly Asian man in a tailored black suit standing in front of the glass-paned entrance. He looks like he might be in his early thirties, but his voice sounds older.

"They've got to go back to the gallery tomorrow for an opening, but I wanted them here for the party. Cordelia invited the artist, but of course she hasn't come. Never can trust the creative, can you?" Even though I'm positive I've never met him before, his smile seems vaguely familiar. "How rude of me. Can I get you a drink?"

"Uh, sure." I watch him cross the room in two long steps and slip behind the bar. "You're . . . Alex, aren't you?" I hesitate slightly on the name, unsure whether or not I should call him "Mr. Tzu." After all, he is a billionaire.

"Very perceptive of you." He fills two highball glasses with ice and selects one of the bottles from the top of the bar. "It's terrible. I've never been able to wean myself off of drinking cognac on the rocks. All that endless prep school training and forced civilization gone to naught. Hope you don't mind." Alex pours out half the bottle, filling both glasses to the brim. "Feel free to throw it in the pool and fix yourself something else." He makes a slight sweeping gesture with his hand at the bottles lined up on the bar.

I walk over and take one of the glasses.

"Alex, I think I should tell you that I'm—"

"Stop!" he cuts me off. "No need to introduce yourself. I'm quite drunk and most assuredly won't remember. . . . A toast?" He holds up his glass. "Well, maybe not . . ." In one swig, he drains half the highball, then leans forward to examine my face more closely in the flickering televised firelight.

I lean back and take a swig of the cognac myself. It's smoother than I expect, and seems to pour straight through my throat and into the bloodstream without ever reaching my stomach.

"Do you like it?" he asks, examining his glass.

"Yes."

"My God, you're svelte as a barracuda in that dress." Alex takes an exaggerated step to the side so that he can take me in.

"Uh, thanks."

"Do you mind if I ask you something terribly personal?"

"It depends."

"Have you tried the deviled eggs?"

"Yes. They were—"

"Where are my manners?" he cuts me off and motions towards a small couch under one of the windows. "Please, have a seat."

Using my left hand to keep my hemline down, I sit tentatively on one side of the couch, while Alex perches himself on the arm across from me. Despite his obvious drunkenness, he sits gracefully, without the least bit of a slouch. Just as I begin to study the unusually high angle of his cheekbones, he smiles and a saberlike canine tooth flashes in his mouth.

"Isabel *Raven*. Not a bad name. I suppose some clerk on Ellis Island shortened it from Ravenowskiovich?"

"Actually, I'm one-thirty-second Chumash Indian. . . . So you know my name?"

"This entire room is filled with your paintings. Do you think I could not know who you are?" He flashes his saber tooth again, then points at an open pack of cigarettes on the end table next to me. "Yours?"

I shake my head, confused.

"They're mine now." Alex reaches out and I hand him the

pack. He offers me one and lights us both up with a yellow Bic that clashes horribly with his otherwise classy attire. "So, Isabel *Raven*, do you ever feel that since the world appears to be on a delusional course, we must develop a delusional approach to the world?"

"Delusional?" I cough, realizing that the cigarette is another Pura Indígena.

"I read it somewhere. I think it's Baudrillard."

"Sounds kind of pretentious," I blurt out before I can stop myself.

"Pretentious? Yes, I guess so. But that doesn't make it any less true."

Most people bristle instantly when you call something they said pretentious, but Alex seems to be able to evaluate the quote objectively, without letting his ego get involved. And in truth, the more I think about the day I've had, the more the world does seem to be on some kind of "delusional course."

"Okay, so how does one go about 'developing a delusional approach to the world'?" I ask.

"Good question." He tilts his head and strokes his stubble-free chin as if in profound thought. "I suppose we could join one of those ludicrous fundamentalist religions that are all the rage these days, but that might interfere with my twin loves of binge drinking and taking the Lord's name in vain."

"So maybe we need to create our own fundamentalist religion," I suggest after a moment's thought. "You know, one specifically dedicated to the fundamentals of binge drinking and taking the Lord's name in vain." I one-up his chin stroking by bending forward and resting my head on my knuckles in imitation of *The Thinker*. "Although personally, I think we should throw chain smoking into the mix and make it a holy trinity."

"Then it's decided, goddamnit!" He French-inhales his cigarette and toasts my cognac highball at the same time.

I wait for him to go on, but he doesn't. Either he's too drunk to notice the conversational lull, or he just doesn't care.

"So . . . why are you buying my paintings?" I finally ask, aiming for a breezy cocktail party tone.

"Because you have more raw talent than Picasso, van Gogh, and Michelangelo combined."

Without thinking, I throw one of my ice cubes at him, miss by a fantastic distance, and watch it sail off somewhere down the hall. Even though I've almost finished the cognac in my glass, I don't feel anywhere near drunk enough to be acting so childish. It's as if something about Alex's presence has suddenly and inexplicably caused me to revert to an adolescent state. When he turns back from watching the ice cube's path down the hall, I feel myself start to blush.

"Can't say I expected that." He raises an eyebrow, but then flashes his saber smile again. His eyes openly acknowledge my hemline for the first time.

"More cognac?" Embarrassed, I hop up and reach for his empty glass.

"Thank you."

I have no idea which of the bottles on the bar is actually cognac, so after filling both glasses with ice from the bucket, I just grab one at random.

"Really, why are you buying my paintings?" I ask again.

"Because I like them. Why else?"

"You actually like them?"

"Oh God, it's Sally Field. You're not one of those self-deprecating artists, are you? Always blinding people with their faux modesty and distracting the world with their unassuming air, while surreptitiously dynamite-fishing for compliments?"

"I don't—"

"I've always thought people should be blatant about their genius. Be able to say, 'I'm not just good, I'm the very best.'"

"Genius?" I bring the now full glasses back.

"Well, okay, maybe not genius, but you really do have a flair for the camp." He takes a sip from his glass, then holds it up to look at it. "What the fuck is this?"

"Fuck if I know."

"The mouth on you." Alex shakes his head. "A misspent youth, no doubt." He takes another sip from the glass, and shrugs in acceptance. "Well, if you really want to know, it's because you're superficial."

"I swear because I'm superficial?"

"No, that's why I'm buying your paintings."

"Oh, thanks."

"I meant it as a compliment."

"And I accept it as an insult."

"Seriously, if there's one thing I've learned from my own excruciatingly superficial life, it's that Los Angeles is about living for the *now*."

Alex finally breaks posture and leans forward to begin gesturing enthusiastically with his hands, spilling what I now can taste is scotch on the sofa. I'm momentarily startled, but there's something so disarming about his face and the slight lisp of his speech that I can't help but drop my guard.

"I mean, that's really what we're all about, isn't it? No one cares about last month's movie, about yesterday's fashion. Not in a town where the actual ground we stand on is in constant tectonic flux."

Alex's childlike enthusiasm somehow serves to complement his almost professorial intensity. "History is for New York or London or Vienna, and the future's for . . . I don't know, say Tokyo. But the present, the *now*, that's here. That's Los Angeles."

"You're pretty passionate about this, aren't you?"

"I mean really, we get so much shit for it. Everybody's always calling Angelenos superficial. Well, you know what? They're right! LA is superficial. It's all about surface—about the sheen of a detailed car, the arc of a fake breast, the flash of a bonded smile. It has no depth. But that's the point now, isn't it?"

"I didn't know there was a point."

"What the hell is wrong with the surface?" Alex continues on undeterred. "The surface of the cake is the icing! And the earth—we live on the *surface* of the earth, don't we? Not down with the fucking mole people!"

"Alright, you definitely lost me with the mole people." With great effort, I manage not to slur this, but the alcohol is definitely starting to hinder my elocution.

"What I'm trying to say is that we're always pissing all over the *now*. Either we're striving for some mythical future where advances in hybrid automobile engines eliminate global warming and end terrorism, or we're floundering in nostalgia for a romanticized family value–packed past that never existed. But the *now*, this precise ephemeral moment, that's what I'm interested in."

"You really believe all that?"

"No." He sighs. "But it's a killer theory, though. Kind of makes me wish I was back at Yale smoking Gauloises and misinterpreting Derrida."

I laugh, but all I can really think about is whether I'm becoming physically attracted to him simply because he likes my paintings, or if there isn't also something seductive in his inebriated intensity. Looking down, I see that my glass is empty again.

"Refill?" Alex is up and heading towards the bar with both glasses. "Which one was it?"

"Was what?"

"Which bottle? What were we drinking?"

I shrug.

"Not particularly observant for an artist, are you?"

"Tell me more about how I'm a genius."

"Back to that again? You really are a one-trick pony." He refills the glasses and hands me one.

I lean back on the couch and take a slug from my highball, only to spit it up a half-second later.

"What? Don't like tequila?" Alex laughs.

I'm about to throw my whole drink at him, but at the last minute recall that he's wearing a five-thousand-dollar suit. I settle instead on another ice cube, which miraculously follows the exact same arc as the first one.

"Pardon my asking, but why do you keep throwing ice down the hall?" He leans towards me, still smiling.

He's only inches away, and I can feel my cheeks start to warm. His smile widens slightly, and of course, out comes his saber tooth again. Something primal overpowers my already inebriated inhibitions, and surprising even myself, I try to kiss him.

"Whoops." He pulls back suddenly, and I have to grab the arm of the couch to keep from face-planting into the floor. "I do believe you're drunk, Ms. Raven."

Utterly mortified, I do my best to drunkenly reposition myself on the couch without my dress riding up. The fact that he's not laughing somehow makes my humiliation even worse.

"You're not really a pedophile, are you?" I finally blurt out, thinking of all the teens hanging around by the pool.

"A what?"

"Everyone at your party is like fifteen years old."

"What are you talking about? It's not *my* party, it's Cordelia's, my daughter. You really are a cheap drunk, aren't you?"

"So you're not a perv?"

"No."

"Gay?"

"No."

"Then why won't you kiss me?" I vaguely realize how arrogant the assumption that any straight male would want to sleep with me is, but up until now, that's been the case. "Are you married?"

"No. Look, you lascivious lush, I'm trying to be a gentleman about this, okay?"

"About what?"

"That sleazeball of a gallery owner told me that you just found out your boyfriend's cheating on you, and that you're probably on the rebound."

"Dahlman actually told you that?" I glance down at the crotch-length cheongsam I'm wearing and, even in my highly inebriated state, am able to put two and two together. "Is that why you bought my paintings? He promised you I'd sleep with you?"

"Actually I bought the paintings for my daughter Cordelia as a birthday present. She thinks you're the next Warhol.... But to be honest, he did suggest something of the sort."

"I'm gonna fucking kill him!"

"Not that he doesn't deserve it, but you should know that it might clip the wings of your Icarus flight to fame. Here, give me your cell phone."

I hand it over, and he plays with it a moment.

"By the way, what's your favorite charity?"

"I don't know … uh, the Sierra Club, I guess." The question catches me off guard.

"Really more of a nonprofit than a charity, but it'll do. I put my number on your phone. Call me when you're sober enough to give legal consent." He hands back the phone and kisses my cheek. "Better go check on the deviled eggs."

"Wait …" I stand up, but Alex has already slipped out the glass door.

The flames on the TV jump over Los Feliz Boulevard and start rolling noiselessly towards the Hollywood Hills. Somewhere, deep in the back of my mind, a voice is whispering for me to have some reaction to my humiliation—to scream, to start crying again, to tear my clothes off and run outside. But my earlier bout of roadside sobbing over Javier has apparently drained the last of my hysterical reserves, so instead I check my cell phone to make sure that he really did give me his number.

Walking over to the bar, I fish in the bucket of mostly melted ice and drop a couple of cubes in the glass. I drain the tequila in two slugs, then refill the glass with gin. This time the liquor does reach my stomach, and hangs there, waiting. It occurs to me that Alex is one of only a handful of men with whom I've had an extended conversation who hasn't at some point told me I need to smile more.

Grabbing the gin, I carry it with me back to the center of the room. The TV finally cuts from views of the fires to an infomercial, and the room goes from red to blue. Trying to hold my glass level, but spilling anyway, I stumble around in a circle, looking at my paintings on the wall. There's "*Venus on the Half*

Shell with Scarlett Johansson," "*Blue Boy* with Macaulay Culkin," and perhaps kitschiest of all, "The Sistine Chapel with James Earl Jones as God and Jamie Foxx as Adam." Despite the fact that they sold for a ridiculous sum of money, that Alex praised them, and that I'm just shy of blind drunk, not a single image is strong enough to counteract the depressive effects of being both dumped and denied in the same day.

I leave the room before making any conscious decision to do so, and I'm out on the lawn staring at an empty glass, unable to remember if I drank any of it or just spilled it all. With the exception of the boy in the black Speedo continuing to swim quiet lap after lap in the empty night, the guests have all left, probably caravanning on to the next party. I catch sight again of the mysterious brick path that leads around to the other side of the deck, and grabbing another deviled egg for the walk, I start down it.

To my surprise, I find that the land does not drop straight off past the deck, but that the path follows a narrow ridge running down into the orange clouds. For a moment, I think I hear laughter up above on the deck, but when I look back, there's no one at the railing.

Almost as soon as I start down the ridge, the path turns to dirt and the light of the party is lost in the mist. Focusing on the ground in front of me, I use exaggerated care to step over the rattlesnake holes and dry rivulets in the increasingly steep trail. The completeness with which the clouds cut me off from the house behind me and the unknown in front of me emphasizes each step to the point of absurdity. I can feel each damp breath of air as it hits my lungs, each beat of my slightly elevated pulse, each tendon of my bare knee brace for each jolt. The scent of wild sage, the rustling of brush as startled rodents scurry off, and the grate of each footstep on the damp sandy soil come to me one at a time, each a separate sensation.

Then, just as I stop thinking about where I'm going, I arrive.

The path comes out of the clouds, and the ridge ends at a small cleared lookout where an old-time brass surveyor's disk has been sunk into the ground to mark the elevation. Beneath the orange shelf of the marine layer, the air is absolutely clear, and I can see the lights of the city spilling out in endless block-by-block repetition across the alluvial plain below. I want to cry out, to bellow a personal challenge to its hideous beauty, but when I open my mouth, nothing comes out.

All of a sudden the empty glass slips from my hand and I realize that it's not just me who's stumbling drunk and unbalanced. The dirt beneath my feet is shifting, rising, falling, crumbling. The brass geological marker moves along with me, its precise calculation lost. I look back out over the city to see the lights twinkle out from another aftershock.

11

I'm a tumbleweed rolling down Hollywood Boulevard—or at least a ghost town version of Hollywood Boulevard. *All of the buildings, from the Cinerama Dome to the Chinese Theatre, have a dusty Spaghetti Western patina, and the wind steadily blowing me down the middle of the empty street whistles with studio-dubbed clarity. I keep trying to scream, but my rustling is drowned out by the artificial wind. Just as I reach the end of the strip, I spot Dahlman sitting on a bus bench, and try to get his attention by pirouetting around in a dust devil.*

"Oh please." He shakes his head in disgust. "Do you have to be so symbolic?"

I awake to the smell of cigarette smoke.

The dream is gone.

Lifting the cushion from on top of my head, I look up at the girl with short bleached-blonde hair staring down at me. She has a beer in one hand, a cigarette dangling out of her mouth, and is wearing a white T-shirt with some Japanese anime character on the front that I've never seen before. Thirteen, maybe.

"Were you choking?" the girl asks.

"Huh?" I jerk the hem of my cheongsam back down.

"I thought you were choking. Drowning in your own vomit or something."

"No."

I feel my head carefully and discover to my partial relief that the pain in the left hemisphere of my brain is hangover-related and not the result of an external blow. When I sit up in the unfamiliar room, I notice that, just like the living room, it's lit only by the TV in one corner. How I managed to get from the overlook back into Alex's house (if this is Alex's house) is a mystery. The girl retreats to a cross-legged position on the far side of the couch, but continues to stare.

"I'm Cordelia," she introduces herself.

"Nice to meet you, I'm—"

"Isabel Raven, I know. Dad told me I might find you passed out somewhere."

"You mean Alex?" I try to compute how Alex could be old enough to have a thirteen-year-old child. Particularly one that looks not the least bit Asian.

"Juan left with somebody else." Cordelia ignores my question.

"Juan? You mean Dahlman?"

"Juan. He told me to tell you. Want a beer?"

"No thanks."

Cordelia pulls a bottle out from somewhere behind the cou anyway and uses the base of a fancy gold lighter to pry it ope notice the bottle has no label.

"I swiped it from the producer who lives next door,"

reassures me. "The fucking bonehead left the side door to his garage unlocked." She dangles the bottle at arm's length across the couch. "Go on, take it."

Too hungover to argue, I lean over to get the beer and by the light of the TV notice strange flecks of black spattered in Cordelia's otherwise green eyes. I take a swig of the beer. It's warm.

"Tastes like . . ." I take another swig.

"Ginseng?"

"That's it."

"I think it's home-brewed. The guy's totally into that New Age Chinese medicine shit. Always begging Dad to give him rhino orn and dried tiger penis. Dad never had the heart to tell him it he's really Dutch-Eskimo."

"Oh." I want to ask the specifics of her relation to Alex, but t think of a tactful way to do it. Turning my attention instead to ickering TV, I make out a familiar-looking character actress in a chair and holding up a plastic gynecological model of nale anatomy. She's aged horribly since I last saw her in a and has the bags of a terminal insomniac under her eyes. ge cuts to a sleazy-looking doctor with botched hair plugs oscene bulge in his surgical scrubs, and then back to the actress.

hat are we watching?" I ask.

rcial." Cordelia finishes her bottle and reaches back ne. "Something about . . . actually, I'm not sure. It's other channel's running doom-and-gloom apocalypse h brushfires."

. I

el like that?" Cordelia suddenly becomes more she your life is some sort of muted infomercial playing endlessly through the night. Like even if you could find the remote and turn up the volume, even if you could sit back in your Barcalounger and finally watch it the whole way through, it would still be about spray-on hair for men or a dog-grooming vacuum cleaner attachment?"

"Not really," I answer after a moment's thought.

"Me neither. It's a killer metaphor, though. Gotta apply to somebody." Cordelia exhales and takes another swig of beer. "So ... you gonna let my dad cornhole you?"

I choke on my beer.

"That's really a lovely way to put it."

"What can I say? I'm dissolute." She winks. "Runs in the family. My grandpa once did ninety days for desecrating a taxidermy shop in Pasadena."

Before I can ask, she cuts me off.

"You really don't want to know. Trust me... Smoke?" Cordelia stuffs the gold lighter in the cellophane and tosses me the pack. "So is it true that you get hornier when you get old?"

"I'm not old." I light up and toss the pack back. To my relief, it's just a Camel Light.

"Yeah, but you're getting there. A couple wrinkles around the eye, having to buy a few of your own drinks at the bar, maybe going on a date with that bald guy from work ... I bet you have a cat."

What the fuck? This girl's relentless.

"No," I lie.

"What are you, like ... twenty-five?"

"Twenty-six," I admit.

Cordelia whistles and shakes her head.

"That's getting up there. Better switch to Egg Beaters."

"What time is it?" I change the subject.

"I don't know. Morning."

"Morning?" I glance around suspiciously at the dark room.

Balancing her beer on the arm of the couch, Cordelia reaches over to the wall and opens a shuttered window. Bright daylight knifes into the room.

"Ack!" I cover my eyes.

"Not too much now. At your age, you've really got to watch those UVB rays." She closes the shutters again. "Hey, so you gonna give me a ride, or what?"

"Where?"

"I've got business at the La Brea tar pits."

"The La Brea tar pits?"

"You know, that's kind of redundant, isn't it? I mean, the word 'brea' means 'tar' in Spanish. So if you say 'La Brea tar pits,' you're basically saying 'The Tar tar pits.' It makes me think of a place where people gather from miles around to dip their fish sticks.... Anyway, it's on your way home if you still live at 824 South Orange Grove Ave. Come on, sleepyhead, I'll drive."

"How do you know where I live?"

"It's on your driver's license." She tosses my cigarette case wallet back to me.

"You stole my wallet?"

"It fell out of your purse while you were sleeping. Fair game. But I did steal the keys to your Nova." She dangles them in front of my face.

"What the hell is wrong with you?" I raise my voice as loud as my hangover will permit.

"Kleptomaniac. Runs in the family. My grandmother lost a hand for it back in the old country." She demonstrates by slashing one hand at the wrist of the other. "Chop chop!"

12

Passing through the living room, I notice that all my paintings are gone (I suppose Alex returned them to the gallery for my show tomorrow). I drag myself outside and, grabbing my clothes from the Nova, change back into my jeans and T-shirt in the now empty asphalt lot. I'm about to toss the dress and shoes into the trunk when I catch sight of the gray picket fence again and, with a sudden change of heart, take a running start and hurl them over.

"Bravo," Cordelia cheers me. "I've always wanted to do that. I just never had the right cheongsam."

"Is your dad still here?" I ask her as we head back towards the Nova.

"He's off doing something or another for charity. Left early this morning."

"Charity?"

"Ever since 9/11, he's been giving money away like Tic Tacs."

"So he was really there?"

"Yes." Cordelia unconsciously bites her lower lip, and for just a moment she seems like an actual thirteen-year-old girl. "Fuck it. Are we going, or what?"

Obviously there's some relief at not having to confront Alex again after making such a fool of myself last night, but there's another part of me that's actually a little disappointed. I decide to go ahead and call him once I get over the hangover.

Twenty minutes later, we're heading south on Fairfax with me chain-smoking, Cordelia driving, and both of us watching the throngs of black-garbed Hasidim strolling home from Saturday morning synagogue. Cordelia hasn't spoken since we left Alex's house, and the longer I sit silently in the passenger seat, the more I begin to wonder why I let a thirteen-year-old who I know for a fact has been drinking behind the wheel of my car. Hungover and humiliated, I seem unable to stop her, and yet I'm not entirely sure I would stop her if I could. There's something so infectious about her anarchistic approach to life that I find myself thinking back to the (admittedly less wild) thirteen-year-old I used to be, and wondering how she'd respond to the rapidly sinking quagmire my world has become.

At the Third Street light, a tricked-out purple Harley pulls up next to the passenger window. The possum-faced boy riding it is even more tricked out in pricey Harley-Davidson accessories than the bike—everything from chaps to fringed leather gloves to an absurd pair of faux vintage goggles. I try not to look at him, but he taps on the window to get me to roll it down.

"Hey, Cordy!" he yells over the roar of his severely chopped muffler.

"How's it hanging, Zach?" Cordelia gives him a nod.

"Can I drop by later?"

"Maybe ... I'll text you."

The light changes and the possum-faced boy's Harley stalls as we pull away.

"Who was that?" I ask.

"Pusher."

"He's your pusher?"

"Zach? Ha!" Cordelia laughs. "No, I push, he pulls."

"So you're a drug dealer?"

"Well, I don't see it as a permanent lifestyle, but it keeps me active ... which reminds me, do you mind if I borrow your gun?" She starts searching under the seats.

"I don't have a gun."

"No?" She pulls out the Blondie eight-track and holds it up to look at it. "Hey, this is worth some money. Can I have it?"

"No." I grab the tape out of her hand. "What do you need a gun for?"

"Intimidation, subjugation, elimination.... Drug dealing's no longer the dancing bear blotter-acid hippie lovefest it was in your day."

Cordelia's cell phone starts playing that "Uncle Fucka" song from the *South Park* movie, and she cuts off at least three cars as she swerves wildly answering it. It's only when she starts speaking that I realize it isn't her phone at all, it's mine. She must have figured out how to change the ringtone.

"Hi there ..." She cuts off another car as she reads the phone screen "... *Juan Dahlman*, what can I do you for?"

"Give me the phone, will you?" I reach for it, but she refuses.

"It's Cordelia.... You were at my birthday party last night? Oh, that *Juan Dahlman* ..." She gives me a lewd wink. " ... right ... so you wanna go get drinks or something? ... Well, I've got meetings all day long, but how's tomorrow for you? ... Great ... Isabel? Oh, she's right here, but too hungover to come to the phone right now. Can I take a message?" Considering she's still three years from getting a driver's license, she does a surprisingly expert job of one-handed parallel parking in one of the metered spots on Sixth Street as she listens. "Right ... right ... So if I come to the show tomorrow, can I get in for free? ... It *is* free? Well, how about a personal VIP tour then? ... Yep ... Fabulous ... See you tomorrow then. Ciao, babe." She hangs up and tosses me the cell phone.

"What was the message?"

"I don't know, something about how you better sign the contract or he'll rip off your head and shit down your throat."

"Well, I'm not signing that contract until I at least get a lawyer to look at it."

"Hey, don't blame me, I'm just the chauffeur."

Cordelia hops out of the Nova and, since she's already stolen all my change from the ashtray, puts a few quarters in the meter.

"Hey, you mind backing me up?" she asks.

"Backing you up?"

"It's worth twenty. Fifty if something goes wrong."

"No way."

"Don't worry. I've been dealing to him for years. The guy's a pussy."

Before I can think of a response, Cordelia takes off like a pronghorn down a footpath into the park. With one eye still blurry from the hangover, I reluctantly follow. The path leads over a little bridge that spans a tar-filled creek, and then wanders out to the lawn in front of the Page Museum. The pylon-shaped structure of the museum rises up from the lawn as a grassy mound until it breaks into crisscrossing black metal beams and a molded concrete frieze that circles the entire building. The frieze seems to tell a story, but one so repetitive that it has no real progression. Sabertooths feeding on mammoths, dire wolves attacking sloth bears, vultures plucking the eyes out of bison, and all of them stuck or about to be stuck in the tar pits. The landscape is depicted as something similar to the African Serengeti, but the seagulls sitting on the black beams above the frieze destroy the effect.

On the lawn itself, a couple of very small girls in AYSO soccer uniforms are weakly kicking a ball back and forth in the noonday sun. Spotting Cordelia near to the museum, I loop around the AYSO girls and head down to the entrance. Despite the fact that it's only a five-minute walk from my apartment, I haven't been here since a fourth-grade field trip, and all I can remember is that the nasty grape Kool-Aid-like stuff they served us made me puke on the bus ride home. Cordelia's waiting for me at the door, and we enter the museum together.

"No no! Closed! *Cerrado*!" a man's voice hits me at the same moment as the air-conditioning.

I shiver involuntarily at the controlled sixty-eight degrees, then shiver again when I look up to see where the voice is coming from. Standing in front of the turnstile is the same bullet-headed triangular man I ran into at the deviled egg bar last night.

"You're not Latino," he adds after a moment, and his face falls from a flush back to a mottled white. "I've been trying to practice my Spanish, you see. Get with the times. Did you know that eighty percent of the world's best new seafood recipes are coming from South America?"

"No." I shake my head.

"It's true."

"Well, Señor Latinophile." Cordelia rises up on her toes in an effort to get in his face. "Did you know that you've got less than a minute to hand over the cash before I give you a Colombian necktie?"

"A Colombian what?"

"It's where I slit your throat and pull your tongue out through your neck."

"That's disgusting."

"I saw it on a *Miami Vice* rerun the other night. It really exists."

"Well then." The man nods and turns to walk away.

"And where the fuck do you think you're going, grandpa?" Cordelia stops him.

"To get the cash. It's in the lab."

"Oh, and what are we supposed to do? Just wait here for you to go grab an AR15 and whack the both of us? I think not. Isabel, watch him." Cordelia jumps the turnstile. The museum forms a square around a central plant-filled atrium, and she heads off to the left.

"Uh, Cordelia? The lab's over there." He points in the opposite direction.

"I knew that!" She changes her course.

Still standing tentatively in the entranceway, I look at the man. If anything, he looks even more condorlike than the night before. Worse yet, he's still wearing the kelly green trousers.

"What's an AR15, anyway?" he whispers.

I give a nervous shrug.

"Hey, I know you! You blew me off at the party last night!" His eyes drop to the V of my crotch, and he frowns. "You changed your clothes."

I nod.

"I don't believe I ever got the chance to introduce myself." He puts out a spade-shaped hand. "I'm Jacques Bonard, acting assistant docent."

Jacques's hand engulfs my own, thumb and all, then gives a surprisingly gentle squeeze.

"Do I seem . . . nervous?" He vigorously nods his bullet head for several beats too long.

"Sorry?"

"It's just I'm sort of new to the game. I mean, I've always been a bit of a shaved fish, if you catch my drift. A few too many years in the back room . . . you know the story. This all must look terrible to you."

"What?"

"My buying illegal prescription drugs in the workplace."

"Oh."

"So do you want a tour?" His neck flexes and unflexes in anticipation.

"I thought you were *cerrado*?"

"Oh that's for the general public. Artists in the midst of a Lance Armstrong race to fame get carte blanche. Besides, the lab's an atrocious mess. It'll take her forever to find that money."

"Aren't I supposed to be watching you?"

"Well, let's just say I start the tour. In order to properly watch me, you'd have to follow me, wouldn't you?" He winks.

Jacques takes a step forward and leans in so close I tense up in expectation of being lifted off my feet. Then, just as suddenly, he turns and goes through the turnstile. When I hesitate, he gestures eagerly with his spade-shaped hand until I follow.

"Here we have the LA High School Mural. Rather drab if you ask me . . . in fact, forget it, forget it entirely, don't even look at it."

He uses the triangle of his chest to block the view and redirect my attention farther down the hall. "Over there we have a magnificently impressive specimen of a California saber-toothed cat, Latin name *Smilodon californicus*. It's the second most common fossil found in the pits, and has recently been declared the state fossil of California. . . ."

Feeling my exit strategy collapse with each step down the hall, I continue following him.

" . . . And this is the 'La Brea Story' multimedia presentation."

"By multimedia presentation, do you mean slide show?"

"Oh Christ, you don't want to see it, do you?"

"No. That's okay."

"A woman after my own heart . . . So I notice you're not wearing a wedding ring. Are you single?"

"I told you last night, I have a boyfriend."

"Sure." He nervously drums the thighs of his kelly green trousers with open palms. "I'm a confirmed bachelor myself. No ball and chain for me. Late-night Yahtzee and Uno games till dawn, if you know where I'm coming from."

"Okay." *I'm going to fucking kill Cordelia for this.*

"So would you say this alleged boyfriend of yours is serious? I mean, are you two . . ." He starts to make an obscene gesture with his spade-shaped hand, then thinks better of it. " . . . involved?"

"Jacques, I really don't feel comfortable talking about this with you."

"Right, right." He nods for far too long, then continues with the tour. "Over here you have more bones." He points to the various animal skeletons on display as we walk. I try to catch the names of some of the bigger ones, but have to sprint to keep up with his yard-long strides. We eventually emerge from the hall into a much larger main room, and the smell of institutional disinfectant that has been exacerbating my hangover suddenly dissipates. "It's all so terribly fascinating … really, terribly.… And here you have a favorite of the kids.…" He stops in front of a large orange drum about four feet high with a flat circular Plexiglas top.

I look down through the top and see that it's divided into four separate compartments full of tar. In each compartment there is a metal bar rising out of the tar, up through the hole in the Plexiglas top, and ending in a handle.

"Go ahead. Try it." Jacques points to the pictograph sign which shows how to lift the handle and reads simply: "ASPHALT IS STICKY: WHAT IT'S LIKE TO BE STUCK IN TAR."

As I pull up on the handle, the tar drags down on the other end, until I finally have to use both hands to get the bar up. The sensation is that of a sucking liquid abyss. It's all too easy to imagine how it would win a war of attrition with an animal.

"Now that would be if your leg only weighed ten pounds. Imagine how hard it would be to lift your leg if you weighed as much as an Imperial Mammoth! Latin name, *Mammuthus imperator*."

"Very hard?"

"You're not kidding.… Oh, come over here. This is one of my favorites. Have you ever wondered what it would be like to actually caress the bones of some long-extinct animal?"

"I can't say that I have." I reluctantly follow Jacques over to a large bone sitting uncovered on top of a pedestal. It has the same dark brown tar-impregnated look as the other ones, but the top is worn shiny where people have touched it.

"Go ahead. It's our 'Hands-on Touch Bone.' You can fondle it as much as you like."

"That's okay." I feel slightly repulsed by the idea.

"No, really, touch it. Touch the bone!" Jacques grabs my hand and starts pulling it towards the display.

"Get off me!" I jerk my hand away.

"Oh!" Jacques seems truly surprised at my reaction. "Was that inappropriate?"

"Completely inappropriate."

"Hey! Everything alright out there?" Cordelia yells from what must be a room behind the wall.

"Yes! Everything's just fine!" Jacques hollers back, then looks at me imploringly. "I'm so sorry.... You see, I'm not..." He struggles for the right word. "... normal."

"I can see that."

"I'm ... I'm very passionate about my work. And well ... it's like I told you, I don't get out much. In fact the last time I had sexual intercourse—"

"WHAT'S THIS?" I actually screech in my fervor to cut him off, then change the subject by pointing to a giant freestanding sloth skeleton.

"Harlan's ground sloth, Latin name *Paramylodon harlani* ..." The tour continues at a rapid pace, as if nothing has happened, and I start to realize that the smell of disinfectant that was so strong in the confinement of the hall is actually emanating from Jacques himself. We move quickly past the small mammal fragments on the far wall, and over to a two-third-sized replica of a mammoth with a mechanical head that cycles between up and down and side-to-side motions. Jacques is already midway into a lengthy explanation about how the electronic mechanisms inside the mammoth would be of specific interest to a painter, when I catch sight of a large yellow wooden box with a tinted glass front.

"What's that?" I interrupt him.

"What? That? Just some woman they found in one of the pits."

"They found a woman? Really?" I move over to the display and look in. It's completely dark. "I can't see anything."

"You have to turn it on. It's set up with a holographic backlighting system."

I watch him stand there with a large smile underlining his bullet head.

"Well, do you think you could turn it on?" I finally ask.

"Why?"

"So I could see it."

"She's only nine thousand years old. Homo sapiens. Doesn't really look any different than us."

"Please?" I flirt as little as possible.

"Okay then." He walks to the back of the display, selects a key from an extending janitorial ring on his belt, and turns it on.

I find myself confronted with a small brown human skeleton. Almost before I can register this fact, a hologram comes up over the skeleton to create the image of a bare-chested Stone Age woman in an animal hide skirt. The woman has dark skin, but her black hair and high cheekbones resemble mine enough to give me the momentary sensation that the rectangular sheet of display glass between us is a mirror. The thought occurs to me that since I'm 1/32nd Chumash Indian, this woman could actually be my ancestor. Another Raven who got trapped in the tar 7000 years B.C., not four blocks from where my own apartment building is currently sinking.

I watch the hologram cycle back and forth between bones and flesh for a while, then Jacques abruptly shuts it off. There's a small sign on the outside of the glass explaining that archaeologists suspect the woman may have fallen victim to foul play, because part of her skull was caved in.

"She was murdered?" I ask when Jacques comes around from behind the box.

"I doubt it. That whole caved-in-skull thing is a bit of a sham. I mean, for all we know an Imperial Mammoth, Latin name *Mammuthus imperator*, stepped on her head while she was sleeping." Jacques puts his spade-shaped hand on my shoulder and propels me bodily over to a wall-sized yellow display case of identical skulls. "Four hundred dire wolf skulls! Latin name, *Canis dirus*."

"Hey! What's going on out there?" Cordelia yells from what must be another hidden room behind the display case.

"Nothing at all! Just giving a tour," Jacques yells back.

"You okay, Isabel?"

"Uh, yeah. I guess so."

"Just holler if he gets out of line, and I'll give him a Guatemalan Cummerbund."

"What's that?" Jacques whispers to me.

I shrug, and he continues the tour.

"They've excavated over sixteen hundred wolf skulls so far. It's the most abundant fossil species we have." Jacques points at the display case. "But sixteen hundred ... well, that would be a ridiculous number to put on display, wouldn't it? So they stuck with just four hundred of the best. Observe the prominent chin, the powerful jaws, the sensuous rising curve of the cheekbones."

When I finally stop thinking about the possible murder of my distant Chumash ancestor and start paying attention to the display, I feel a wave of uneasiness ripple through me. Despite the fluorescent backlit glow, there's something so primitive about stacking row upon row of dead animal skulls that it seems more primal than paleontological.

"What happened to the bodies?" The thought suddenly occurs to me.

"What bodies?"

"Of the wolves. You have the skeletons, but what happened to the flesh?"

"It mostly just rotted away. At least what the birds didn't eat."

"So it's still in the tar?" I think of La Brea Woman again.

"Of course not. Like I said, the flesh decayed a long time ago." Jacques flexes his neck in annoyance at so stupid a question.

"Right, but whatever it decayed into, that's still in the tar, isn't it?"

"Would you like to have lunch with me?" Jacques throws a curveball.

"What?"

"I brought a sandwich from home. We could split it." He pulls a mashed brown blob sealed in a Ziploc bag from the front pocket of his kelly green trousers. "It's chipped beef on pumpernickel."

Just in time, Cordelia reappears through a hidden door that's flush with a chronological mural of the Los Angeles Basin. She's tucked her jeans into her cowboy boots, and I notice immediately by the odd sharp bulges around her calves and ankles that there's something stuffed in her pant legs.

"That lab's a fucking mess." She tosses a large pill bottle to Jacques, then pulls me away and starts rushing towards the exit. "We gotta motor. If you need any more of those roofies, Jacques, you just text me."

"Wait!" Jacques calls after me. "What about lunch?"

14

Cordelia stops at the top of the stairs once we're outside.

"What's in your pants?" I ask.

"Awfully forward, aren't you?" She laughs.

"I'm serious."

"Bones bones bones and more bones. They were all over the place. I even got a velociraptor knee."

"Velociraptor? They never found any dinosaurs in the tar pits."

"Huh? Oh, I see. You take a ten-minute tour and now you're the be-all and end-all of asphalt excavation." Cordelia scouts out the grassy expanse next to the museum. "Okay, we go separately. I take the high road, you take …" She points to the clump of trees behind the County Art Museum. "We meet up at the car in fifteen minutes. And don't run. Just meander on back to the car like there's nothing wrong. That way if they catch us on security cameras, we won't look suspicious at trial."

"Jesus Christ, Cordelia! At trial? How many did you steal?"

Cordelia is already attempting to make her painful bowlegged walk look casual as she heads up towards the Sixth Street sidewalk. Not wanting to be an accomplice, I consider making a run for the car and ditching her, but realize that she has the car keys, and for that matter, my apartment keys too.

I'm about thirty feet down the path and just past the AYSO girls still weakly kicking the soccer ball, when a woman wearing a trucker's hat and blue jeans starts heading straight for me. Paranoia tells me I've been caught, but logic tells me that she's coming from the opposite direction of the Page Museum. It's only when I'm within hailing distance that I realize it's the one-legged woman from Dahlman's gallery.

"Hey . . ." I still can't call her Peg.

"Isabel! You're up early. I thought artists never rose before noon." She hands me a juice box from a minicooler she's carrying.

"Thanks." I take the box, not knowing what else to do. "So, why are you . . . ?"

"Underprivileged kids at LACMA." She points to the County Art Museum next door. "Luan volunteered to do table duty, but got an epic case of the trots. I'm guessing it was the abalone. Why anyone would eat that gelatinous shit is beyond me."

"Oh . . ." I'm not sure if Luan is her friend or lover (or for that matter, male or female).

"And why are you down here so bright and early?"

"Well, actually . . ." Not wanting to incriminate myself, I widen my eyes slightly like a thought just hit me, and change the subject. "So is Dahlman really flipped out about me not signing the contract?"

"No clue, I've been here all morning." Peg shakes her head,

and I can hear the faint hissing of her artificial leg working. "Hey, by the way, I'm sorry about Javier. I guess it was bound to happen, but I still think he's a pig fucker."

"What about Javier?"

"You haven't heard?"

"What?"

"Wow." Peg takes an exaggerated swipe at her forehead. "This is awkward. It's probably best if you talk to him yourself—you know, at least hear him out."

"Just tell me, okay?" It's all I can do to keep from throttling her.

"He's engaged to Mirabel Matamoros."

"What are you talking about? She's like sixteen!"

"Sixteen and three months to be precise. They have a picture of her birth certificate on that Web site *The Smoking Gun*. It's in the section with all the court documents from her emancipation trial last year."

"I can't fucking believe this … I just talked to him yesterday!"

"What did he say?"

"He said …" Obviously in retrospect, the fact that he admitted to sleeping with her should have been a heads-up. "Never mind what he said. I just … I just can't believe how fucked up my life is."

"You should put it in perspective. It could be a whole lot worse."

"How?"

"Did you hear about that guy out on the beach in Santa Monica last night when the aftershock hit?"

I shake my head.

"Apparently during an earthquake sand can temporarily become as fluid as water. It's a process called liquefaction. Anyway, this guy was just standing there on the beach when the quake hit and the sand liquefied. He got buried alive up to the neck." Peg brings her free hand up to her own neck in demonstration. "But that's not the worst of it. Since it was the middle of the night, nobody was there to hear his screams. He was stuck for hours as the morning tide slowly crept up and drowned him."

"Okay, you're right. That is worse."

"Hey, if you think that's bad, you should hear what happened to the cleaning woman on the forty-seventh floor of the old Security Pacific building. The entire—"

Before she can finish, Peg's cell rings and she holds up a finger while she checks the number.

"Crap … I'm sorry, I have to take this." She answers and takes a few hissing steps away from the table for privacy.

Realizing that I really don't want to know what happened to the cleaning lady, I tap my forearm where a watch would be if I had one, give Peg a wave, and drop down to the path that runs next to the giant Lake Pit in order to cross the lawn.

The pit is swollen to a point it usually reaches only after the rains, and the tar has broken from its normal state of absolute blackness to form oily rainbows in places. Littered around the sides are the bottles, cans, and sticks that people have thrown over the fence, trying to sink a piece of their present into history. Every now and then a furious bubbling of methane gas breaks the surface, and then slowly subsides. The only other person in the park actually looking at the tar is a small Filipino boy, both hands clasped firmly to the Cyclone fence, who's staring at the methane bubbles and crying.

Feeling seriously dehydrated from the previous night's drinking, I stab the little straw into the juice box Peg gave me and take a sip.

It's fucking horrible. When I look at the label, I see that it's carrot-pear. For a moment, I consider tossing it into the tar along with the other trash to baffle future researchers studying early twenty-first-century culture, but I go with the conveniently placed fifty-gallon drum garbage can instead.

Before I can make it another ten feet down the path, my cell phone goes off. When I check the number, I see from the 415 area code that the call's from San Francisco. Not having any friends or family left in the Bay Area, I consider not answering, but then do.

"Hello?"

"*Is this Isabel Raven?*" a male voice asks.

"Maybe. Who's this?"

"*This is Eric Garcia. I'm the executive director of the Sierra Club—*"

"I'm sorry, but I already gave this year," I cut him off.

"*Oh …*" He seems a little taken aback. "*Actually, that's what I'm calling about. I wanted to thank you personally on behalf of everyone here. A donation this generous will help us enormously both in our ongoing effort to—*"

"A hundred bucks is gonna go that far?" I cut him off again.

"*A hundred … ? Actually, Ms. Raven, the donation we received in your name this morning was for one million dollars.*"

"A million dollars? Is this some kind of joke?"

"*Uh … no. It's not a joke, Ms. Raven, we—*"

"Look, I don't know who pledged that money, but obviously there's no way in hell you're going to get a million dollars out of me. I can't even—"

"*I'm sorry.*" This time he cuts me off. "*But there must be some mistake. We already have your donation. It was delivered this morning to our Los Angeles office as a cashier's check.*"

"So basically what you're saying is that I just donated a million dollars to the Sierra Club?" I suddenly recall Alex's question last night as to my favorite charity … not to mention the fact that Cordelia said he was doing something charity-related this morning.

"I assure you, Ms. Raven, it's no joke. I'm not sure how—"

I hang up and use the speed dial to call the number Alex programmed in.

"Hey, Isabel, how's the hangover?"

"I feel like boiled mutton. Did you by any chance donate a million dollars in my name to the Sierra Club?"

"Possibly. It's been a busy morning."

"Is this normal billionaire behavior or are you totally nuts?"

"Six of one, a baker's dozen of the other. Actually, everyone in my family is given to wildly extravagant romantic gestures … or at least Cordelia is."

"I'd say 'wildly extravagant' is something of an understatement. You might want to consider prefacing it with a couple 'megas' or 'ultras.' Seriously, how'd you get the donation in my name?"

"Ancient Chinese Internet secret … Actually, it was easy." There's an uncharacteristic pause in his generally slick banter. *"I'm glad you called."*

"It was the least I could do, given the psychopathic nature of your philanthropy."

"Are you okay? You sound kind of … I don't know, tense?"

"You know what you said last night about needing a 'delusional approach' to the world?"

"Yes."

"Well, it sounds better than ever."

"Is this about that cleaning woman in the old Security Pacific building or about Javier pulling a Federline?"

"You heard about Javier? What? Did they put out a press release or something?"

"Two, actually. The second one mentioned you by name as 'a pasty old white bitch who puts naked puta *pictures of herself on the Internet.'"*

"Do you think it would be too dramatic for me to jump in a tar pit?" For some reason, I think of La Brea Woman, and wonder if this is the pit where they found her.

"As a recently jilted artist rumored to be involved with an eccentric billionaire, yes, I think it would."

"Figures. Hey, now that I'm sober enough to give consent, I don't suppose you happen to have time to make out with me?" Somehow the question sounded less brazen in my head.

"You truly are the master of genteel euphemism.... Actually, I'd love to, but I'm supposed to have lunch with Cordelia. She's been, well, acting out a little lately. I'm trying to get her to see a shrink."

"Oh." Obviously, I should tell him what just happened, but I don't. "Anything I can do?"

"That's okay. But thanks for the offer. How about a rain check on the proposed debauchery? Say ... tonight?"

"Sure."

I hang up and watch the methane bubbles a little longer to try and sort out my head. Unfortunately, my thoughts keep drifting from Alex to a disturbing image of Mirabel crying at the altar in her blood-spattered Vera Wang wedding bikini, while I use a Louisville Slugger to take batting practice at Javier's head. After a minute or two, I give up on the head sorting and start again along the path until I reach the shelter of the California oaks and cut across the grass up towards Sixth Street. Before I'm ten feet off the path, an old Armenian woman with a black scarf over her head starts yelling at me from one of the park benches. Since she isn't yelling in English, I try to ignore her and take a couple more steps before realizing what she's actually yelling about. The grass under the trees is spotted with little pools of black, a few of the bigger ones marked with orange traffic cones, but most not. The tar has not only risen in the Lake Pit, but is starting to seep out into the grass as well.

I stop abruptly and turn to look at the Armenian woman. Slowly, as if explaining something to a child, she lifts her right index finger to her right cheek and pulls it down in a gesture that makes her eyeball appear much larger. It's the same gesture that the parking attendant at Musso's made.

By the time I reach the car, Cordelia has already taken off her jeans and is shaking their contents into the Nova's trunk.

"What the hell?" I confront her.

"Well, I can't very well walk around with bones in my jeans, can I now?"

"Doesn't this make me an accessory or something?"

"There's a ground sloth femur in it for you if you keep quiet."

"What if I don't want a ground sloth femur?"

"Then take one of these." She hands me a four-inch hooked claw. It's stained brown by the tar, but is still surprisingly sharp. "Just remember the saber teeth are mine. I got at least seven of them and I want to make a necklace." She pulls on her jeans and steps back into her cowboy boots. "Look. What's done is done. Just get in the car and drive before that freak of nature gets wise and calls the cops."

"What about you?" I pocket the claw.

"Me? I'll walk. I'm supposed to meet Dad for lunch at Canter's. He seems really concerned about me lately."

"With good reason!"

"Remember. The saber teeth are mine." She tosses me my keys.

15

Back at the San Maximón Arms, the police and fire trucks are gone, but the yellow police tape blocking the entrance to the building remains. In the closed second-floor kitchen window of my apartment, I can see my cat Jello pathetically nudging the pane in an attempt to escape.

That settles it.

I walk straight up to the propped-open front door, duck under the yellow tape, and, trying my best to breathe through my mouth, enter. The extreme tilt of the stairwell makes the climb upstairs something of an acrobatic maneuver, and I soon resort to crawling on my hands and knees. One look at the second-floor hall and it's obvious that the building is not long for this world. In addition to the maze of cracks and warped flooring, a major fissure more than an inch thick bisects the structure into two precariously joined halves. Just the weight of my body walking down the hall causes the building to sink noticeably deeper into the tar.

When I reach the door of my apartment, I hear Jello crying frantically behind it, but the collapsing doorframe has splintered it stuck. I try to shove the door open with my shoulder a few times, then stub my toe attempting to do the front kick I learned in my undergrad Take Back the Night self-defense course.

"Need some help?" Chris appears at the stairwell.

"What are you doing here?"

"George McClure in 1C paid me a grand to rescue his stamp collection. Did you know he has half a sheet of those upside-down airplanes?" Chris spins an impressive full roundhouse kick at the door and it shatters inward.

"Nice kick."

"At least I learned something useful during my horribly exploited childhood." He examines the collapsing doorframe. "This sucker's gonna drop any time now. You're lucky your dad came by earlier to clean the place out."

"My dad?"

Chris nods.

Considering that in the four years I've lived here, my father has never even visited, this seems exceedingly odd, but then it's not out of character for my father to do things completely out of character. Initially frightened by the door being kicked in, Jello has regained her courage, and tries to make a run past me out the door. Fortunately, Chris manages to catch her by the scruff of the neck and lift her. Jello claws madly at the air for a moment, then gives up and goes limp.

"A second childhood trick. We used cats painted like white tiger kittens on *Karate*," he explains. "Do you have a pet carrier?"

I run (actually, with the tilt of the floor, it's more of an aggressive hobble) into the bedroom to get the cardboard carrying case out of the closet, noticing along the way that the only things my dad bothered to take were my paintings. Even the antique Tiffany lamp that Javier's manic-depressive grandmother gave me for a birthday present is still sitting on the bedside table … and why would he leave poor Jello? I grab the lamp and carrying case and head back to the living room.

"Here you go, kitty." Chris opens the case and manages to stuff Jello in without receiving a single scratch.

By the time we make it back outside, the building has already sunk another two inches into the tar. Since the lawn is dotted with tar seeps, we head all the way to the curb before stopping.

"Smoke?" Chris pulls a new pack of Pura Indígena from his jumpsuit pocket.

I take the cigarette and light it off one of his kitchen matches. As soon as I inhale, large green splotches begin to move across my field of vision. I try to keep looking at him, but the green is alternately covering either his blue jumpsuit or his tapired face, both of which are somehow essential to actually seeing him.

"What the hell is with these cigarettes?"

"They are kind of strong, aren't they? One of the Mexican landscapers working on that new building down the block told me they have lead in them. *Plomo*. I had to look it up."

"Lead?"

"He said in Mexico only campesinos smoke them." Chris checks his watch. "Hey, I gotta get a move on it. *Miami Vice* is on in ten minutes. They're showing reruns on cable twice a day now. Luckily my mom only lives three blocks from here, so I can watch it there. Don't suppose you want to come with?"

"No thanks … but speaking of parents, did my dad say if he was taking my paintings to the gallery?"

"Nope. As a matter of fact, he didn't say much of anything. Just took the paintings and a couple pairs of underwear from the floor."

"He took my ... he took my underwear?"

"Yeah. Imagine a dad willing to do his daughter's laundry."

"Wait ... what did he look like?"

"I don't know ... Kind of a doughy build with a gray ponytail." Chris glances at his watch again. "Shit. Gotta run."

Dahlman.

16

I half expect (as I always do) for my old bedroom to be covered with the concert flyers and punk rock posters of my youth, but the week I left for college was the same week my mother first discovered IKEA. With the exception of a charcoal sketch hanging over the bed of Brad Pitt embracing Angelina Jolie in Klimt's *The Kiss*, everything in the room is either blond wood or molded white plastic, creating such a state of Scandinavian sterility that I unconsciously start humming ABBA. Despite the fact that I'm the only person who ever stays over, it has officially been redubbed the guest room. In the back of a closet now filled with my mother's long-retired "East Coast" winter clothes (and a cowering Jello), I find a black dress I wore to a Christmas party two years ago and never took home. It was too small back then, but when I shower and change into it, the thing fits like a sackcloth.

Using a plastic window planter and a bag of organic potting soil from the garage, I do my best to make Jello a litter box, and then put a blob of grass-fed ground beef (which she loves, but occasionally pukes up) in a cereal bowl. Since Jello won't be coaxed out of the closet, I filth the Swedish immaculateness of my bedroom by leaving them in front of the closet door.

Considering the morning I've had, I figure I better try to take it slow and lie down, but that turns out to be easier said than done. My legs are so restless that I have to keep shifting position every few seconds, and when I force myself to keep them still, my left eye starts twitching. As if that's not bad enough, I've got so many voices chattering in my head—Dahlman, Javier, Mirabel, Cordelia—that my own internal monologue has been more or less drowned out. It's like trying to use a leaf blower during a hurricane.

In the bookshelf/bedside table, I find a mammoth coffee table book with reproductions of paintings in the Louvre, and drag it up onto the bed to read. Unfortunately, all the copycat painting I've been doing has made paging through a "greatest hits" of European art feel more like work than pleasure, and I can't help thinking up new kitschy celebrities to pair with the paintings. I stuff the Louvre book back in the bedside table and pull out a magazine, but the first page I turn to has the same "LOOSE LIPS SINK SHIPS" vaginal rejuvenation ad that Dahlman showed me at Musso's.

"Honey, are you going to be here for dinner?" My mother peeks her head in the open bedroom door. "I'm making Irish stew."

"That sounds great."

"Your father doesn't like parsnips, though, so I'm leaving them out.... I suppose I could make two pots, if you really like parsnips."

"That's fine, I hate parsnips too.... Mom, can I ask you something?"

"What's that?" She steps all the way into the bedroom.

"Back when you were a writer … did you ever feel pressure to sell out?"

"Sell out? No … not that I recall. Of course, pre–*Harry Potter* there wasn't all that much money in children's books anyway."

"Dahlman wants me to do a vaginal rejuvenation ad."

"Oh!" She laughs. "Well, I suppose there's nothing wrong with helping women regain confidence in their coochies."

"Right …" I decide not to debate this point with her. "But don't you think it's kind of vulgar?"

"I suppose so." She pauses to think about it. "But really, haven't the arts always been vulgar? I mean, when I think back to all the publishing industry dick I sucked in the early seventies trying to get my books out there …" She shakes her head and lets out a low whistle. "Actually, the trick is to take a deep breath, relax your throat, and just—"

"Mom!"

"What?"

Fortunately her cell phone rings before I have to explain, and she leaves the room to answer it. I make a mental note to never talk about my career with my mother again.

Having failed to relax reading the offerings of the bookshelf/bedside table, I decide to give TV a try. The den (which despite the fact that it contains only a single squat bookcase, my parents insist on calling the "library") has a better TV than my bedroom, so I head in there, create a nest of throw pillows in order to defeat the fashionably angular couch, and hit the remote. Looking for suitably mindless entertainment, I jump to the music video channels. The first has Mirabel Matamoros hosting what looks like some sort of beach-themed antidiscrimination party (wearing a bikini that would make a samba queen blush), and the second is showing "Mirabel Matamoros: High Rolling Teen," in which her bikini is so small they actually have to digitally blur out the occasional nipple or wayward labia.

Goddamnit. Can't somebody buy that fucking slut a pareo?

I flip off the TV and head back into the bedroom to grab my cell phone. Considering I just met him last night and we haven't even kissed yet, it would be way too needy of me to call Alex again so soon. But then again, dropping a million-dollar cashier's check on the Sierra Club in my name doesn't exactly point to him as playing it Steve McQueen cool either. I end up hitting the speed dial despite myself.

"*Are you watching this Mirabel Matamoros thing on the Celeb Network?*" he answers.

"How many channels can she be on at once?"

"*According to TiVo, that would be six.*"

"You know she's a Mormon."

"*Really?*"

"Well, a lapsed Mormon at least."

"*Oh shit . . . can you hold on a second?*"

"Sure."

He muffles the phone, but I can hear him arguing with someone in the background.

"*Sorry, back again.*" He takes his hand off the receiver. "*It's just I need to sell this house by tomorrow, and the real estate guy keeps talking to me about relandscaping for 'curb appeal.'*"

"Why do you need to sell your house?"

"*Because it's butt-ugly, that's why. You've seen it.*"

I can't argue with that.

"So then why'd you buy it in the first place?"

"*You're going to laugh, but I bought it over the Internet. I don't know what the hell I was thinking. Never buy a house over the Internet. In fact, never buy anything over the Internet. I fucking hate the Internet.*" This seems rather odd advice, coming as it does from a tech boom billionaire.

"Okay." There's an awkward pause as I try to think how best to phrase what I really called about. "So . . . any chance I'm gonna get lucky tonight?" I finally ask.

"*Can't speak for your other prospects, but unfortunately I've gotta try and find Cordelia. She never showed up at Canter's for lunch, and the police were here looking for her again.*"

My stomach drops as I think about the bones still crammed in the trunk of the Nova.

"Did they say why they want to talk to her?"

"*No. They just said she's 'wanted for questioning.'*"

"Alex . . ." I finally feel comfortable enough to just blurt it out. "How come you have a thirteen-year-old daughter who looks nothing like you?"

"*I was wondering when you were going to ask that.*" He laughs. "*She's adopted.*"

"So you're playing Daddy Warbucks or something?"

"*Actually, she's my business partner's daughter.*" His voice changes.

"Oh." Sensing something's wrong, I decide not to follow up.

"*He died at the World Trade Center.*"

"Wow. I'm sorry."

"*We'd been up all night in the South Tower hammering out the details of another IPO when the American Airlines plane hit the North Tower. Most of us decided to get the fuck out of there, but David had a new DV camera that he'd bought the day before at B&H, and wanted to film the fire.*" Alex's voice has shifted to an almost robotic monotone. *"The last thing I heard him say as I ran for the elevator was 'Holy shit! They're jumping.'"*

There's a pause as I try and fail to come up with an appropriate response. The cell connection is remarkably clear for my parents' house, and I can hear him breathing on the other end of the line.

"I walked all the way back to my suite at the Plaza covered in dust, and spent the next four days in a daze watching CNN.... Then Cordelia showed up. Since the airlines weren't flying, she'd somehow convinced the gardener and nanny to take turns at the wheel and drive her all the way out from LA."

"Alex ..."

"All four of us took to watching CNN and living off room service. I don't know how many days went by ... maybe weeks, but eventually that fucker Bush came on TV to make an announcement. Cordelia had lost her father, I'd lost my best friend and business partner, and the nanny was still trying to find out what happened to her cousin who'd worked as a busboy in Windows on the World. We were all just sitting there in total shock and not knowing what to do, when Bush comes on with that sickening little smirk of his, and tells us to be brave and go shopping."

Again, I can't think of anything to say.

"Anyway, that's when I decided to adopt Cordelia. It seemed liked the least I could do." He takes a deep breath, and his voice returns to something approximating normal. *"Look, I know Cordelia's fucking up. But I mean, if you had to go through what she did, you'd fuck up too."*

"Alex, I ... I don't know what to say."

"I'm okay, really, it's Cordelia I'm worried about. I'm pretty much at a loss as to where she could be, but I'm going to call some of her friends and see if I can't track her down. I'll talk to you tomorrow, okay?"

"Okay."

Way to play the seductress.

I end up watching *Boogie Nights* on DVD, which for some reason is wedged in the squat bookcase between Virginia Woolf and Chuck Palahniuk. I'm done with the movie and in the midst of watching the "Special Features" footage of Mark Wahlberg's prosthetic penis when my mother calls out for dinner.

Despite all the windows being open, the kitchen is filled with smoke. It takes me a second to realize that actually it's not *despite* the open windows, it's because of them. The Santa Anas have picked up and are blowing in smoke from the fires.

My father is watching the minuscule Sony TV on top of the counter. He glances up when I walk in.

"How's it going, Dad?"

"Still the end of the world." He smiles. "But it looks as if they've got the fire under control." He points to the Sony, then offers me a hit off his joint.

"No thanks."

"You sure? Dinner's almost ready."

The same reporter who tried to interview me at my apartment appears on the TV screen in front of a fire crew. She blinks twice and starts to move her mouth, but there's something wrong with the audio feed, and no sound comes out. All around her jackrabbits, squirrels, and even a few deer are sprinting past to get out of the fire's way. When the sound does kick in, it's out of synch with the images.

" ... *more than three dozen homes destroyed in Glendale alone. Now with the fires in the Los Feliz neighborhood—home to many*

A-list, but unpretentious celebrities—fear has struck the heart of the entertainment industry."

"Dinnertime!" my mother calls from the stove. "Turn off the idiot box."

With no remote in sight, I reach over to click off the TV, then sit down. As usual, my mother has cooked enough to feed a lumberjack crew, and puts down a lobster pot filled with what must be two gallons of Irish stew. I eat three oversized bowls in silence while my parents discuss the new www.pinballapocalypse.com Web site my mother's setting up to help promote my father's doomsday theory. It's only after everyone's finished and my father pulls a bottle of Cuervo tequila off the counter to pour us each a shot that I speak.

"Mom, Dad, I think . . . well, I'm fairly sure that I'm becoming unhinged."

"No you're not, honey." My mother pats my hand. "It's just that you're an introvert born into a ridiculously extroverted world."

"Actually, I think it might be more than that."

"Really?" My unflappable father knocks back the tequila and pours himself another. "Back when I was doing contract work for the Air Force, one of the lieutenant majors turned out to be unhinged. He started doing this weird thing with his eyes. He'd crinkle the left one up very small so that only a slit was showing, and raise the eyebrow over the right eye so that it opened up all the way. Then he kind of tilted his head to the side and limped around the parade ground yelling 'Arrrgh!' like a pirate. Turned out he was a chronic masturbator escaped from the VA. You aren't masturbating too much, are you?"

"Define 'too much.'"

"Your father's right." My mother knocks back her tequila shot. "You should stop choking the chicken."

"Well, I did meet someone new last night."

"Really?" My mother does an excited little hop in her chair. "What's he or she like?" she asks with gender-neutral élan.

"*He* is a billionaire."

"Nobody's perfect." My father shrugs.

I knock back my own shot of tequila and look at both of them. For some reason I think of Cordelia.

"I don't mean to be rude," I ask. "But am I in any way biologically related to either of you?"

"Don't be a sillyhead." My mother pours me another shot of tequila. "Is this about that vaginal rejuvenation ad Dahlman wants you to do?"

"Of course it's about the VR ad. That and the fact my apartment building is sinking into a tar pit, there are naked photos of me all over the Internet, and my boyfriend is marrying a sixteen-year-old ... Oh, not to mention the fact that the trunk of my car is filled with priceless stolen bones and I'm probably going to jail for the rest of my life."

"At least you're better off than that cleaning woman in the old Security Pacific building." My father holds out his glass for my mother to pour him a third shot.

"Somehow that's not particularly comforting."

"Well then just remember that since the world will spin out of its orbit and collide with the moon in 2049, in the long run, there really isn't a long run."

"Oh hush, honey!" My mother pats his forearm.

"You know that's a pretty fucked-up thing to tell your daughter," I counter.

"I'd say it's pretty fucked up in general, no matter who you tell." My father nods.

After dinner, I hunt around for Jello until I find her hiding behind the dryer and drag her back to my old bedroom. Using the IKEA torchlight for the first time, I notice that black earthquake cracks have crawled their way up the walls and onto the ceiling. I think about calling Alex again, but then think better of it. Looking up, I spot my charcoal sketch of Angelina and Brad entwined in *The Kiss* above the bed. Why can't I just have casual fuck friends like Angelina used to?

I use the remote to turn on the retro egg-shaped TV in the corner. The cable must have gone out in the wind, because snow is flickering on every channel. All of a sudden, the heavy meal combines with the tequila to make me exhausted despite the early hour. Without taking off my dress, I climb under the white comforter and fall asleep to the gentle rocking of the Santa Anas.

17

I'm high up in the mountains of Central America surrounded by cloud forest on all sides. *Rebel soldiers are running every which way with AK–47s in their hands and red bandannas over their faces. They say nothing, but I can see the terror in their eyes as they wordlessly pass by. Down below, an unseen army is firing up at us, and bullets whiz by, slamming into the massive trees. Despite all this, I feel remarkably calm, almost happy. The thin high-altitude air and gently blowing white mist give everything a fairy-tale glow, as if the monkeys and toucans scurrying around up in the treetops are going to come down and tell me the secrets of the forest.*

I bum a cigarette off one of the passing rebels, and start down a narrow red mud path that's crisscrossed with tree roots so large I occasionally have to use my hands to climb over them. The path winds through the forest until it reaches a small clearing where a rebel encampment is under siege. Bullet-riddled corpses litter the ground, and dozens of wounded lie bleeding to death in the mud while those still alive shoot back at the unseen army in a desperate attempt not to be overrun. Strangely, even the wounded are silent.

To my surprise, Javier steps out from one of the rebel huts smoking a cigar and sporting a ridiculous Che Guevara beard.

I start to laugh.

"You think this is funny?" He pulls the pin on a hand grenade and tosses it down the hillside at the enemy to emphasize his point. "People here are literally dying for a cause."

"What cause?"

"That's not the point." He grabs an AK–47 from one of the passing rebels, racks the slide, and aims it at my head. "The point is, you were never faithful to me. Not where it counts."

"That's not true."

"The truth hurts, Isabel." He pulls the trigger.

I wake up with a start when Jello leaps off the white IKEA particle board dresser and cannonballs onto my stomach. She immediately starts squawking for attention, and feeling guilty, I pet her while I try to figure out what the hell my dream meant. Fifteen minutes later, I'm none the wiser, and Jello begins to chew on my hand to signal she's had enough. I get up and change out of the dress and back into my T-shirt and jeans.

For some reason, it isn't until I start brushing my teeth that the preshow jitters kick in. With all the crazy shit that's been going on the last couple of days, I'd actually managed to more or less put the opening out of my mind. But now every little ounce of stored-up fear and anxiety slams into me like a quadruple shot of espresso. *Why the hell didn't I buy a fresh pack of cigarettes?*

When I walk into the kitchen, my mother almost gives me a heart attack by screaming "Congratulations!" and hugging me so hard I feel my floating ribs start to give.

"For what?" I ask, trying to breathe.

"You made the cover!"

She breaks her grasp and leads me over to the table, where the *Calendar* section is lying on top of the Sunday paper. And there I am. Taking up the full page in the blue cheongsam that Dahlman made me wear. It is without doubt the best photo anybody has ever taken of me ... and for the life of me I can't remember who took it or when. I'm standing next to Alex's rotting gray fence with the convecting orange clouds stretching out over the city behind me. Obviously the *L.A. Times* photographer must have been at Alex's party, but I'm positive I was never actually introduced.

"For once you smiled!" my mother chirps.

I look again. It's true, I am smiling. I must have been blind drunk.

"Your father's down at the Mexican bakery. Refined carbs be damned, we're eating *pan dulce*!"

I end up having an impromptu celebratory breakfast of Mexican pastries and about two pounds of serrano ham that my mother has left over from her annual Don Quixote party. Both Armando Chevre and my ex–porn star neighbor Vanessa stop by, as well as Horst Zenner, an independently wealthy documentary filmmaker who recently moved into the geodesic dome on Chula Loma. Obviously I'm more than a little conflicted about being celebrated simply because I take a good photo instead of for my art, but then again it's a hell of a lot better than being celebrated for a vaginal rejuvenation ad. With even Horst's German short-haired pointer puppy showing enthusiasm, I can't help but join in.

"You know, I once made the cover of the *L.A. Times*," Armando leans across the kitchen table to brag. According to his exceptionally outdated (and yet apparently effective) fitness strategy, he only drinks alcohol before 11 A.M., and it's obvious by his breath that he's been hitting my father's single malt. "And not just the *Calendar* section either. I was front page!"

"More *jamón*?" Vanessa distracts him with the ham before he can launch into a story. Armando's drunk enough that the technique works, and she comes over to sit next to me. "Isabel, darling, congratulations!"

"Thanks, Aunt Vanessa. How are you?" It seems a little ridiculous to be a grown woman and still call her "Aunt Vanessa," but I'm afraid she'll be offended if I stop.

"Proactively recentered as always." She winks. "But what about you? Nervous about the big show?"

"Uh . . . a little."

"Need a Klonopin? I think I've got some in my purse. . . ." She starts rooting around in her enormous bag, looking for it.

"No thanks. I'm good."

"You sure?" She pulls out an orange prescription bottle and rattles it to tempt me.

"Yeah. That stuff just knocks me out."

"Really? I pop them like freakin' Altoids." Vanessa winks again, then drops the bottle back into the bag. "So then . . . how's the love life?" Reaching under the table, she actually pats my crotch.

"Uh . . ." Considering she's an ex-porn star (not to mention the person who gave me my first vibrator at age eleven), I shouldn't be embarrassed, but of course I am. "Not so great at the moment."

"Well, if you find you need professional help, I can give you the number of someone truly fabulous. He's gotten me through a lot of hard times." She relinquishes my crotch and squeezes my thigh instead.

"What, like a shrink?"

"Oh no . . ." She laughs. "More like a gigolo. I swear, the guy's got a tongue that would put Gene Simmons to shame." She demonstrates by wagging her own tongue around in a disturbingly lizard-like fashion, then gets up to go talk to my mother.

With Armando now attempting to play footsie with me under the table, I use the opportunity to get up too and try and find where Jello has chosen to hide from Horst's overly inquisitive German short-haired pointer puppy. The search eventually leads me into the attached garage, where I find not only Jello hiding under the Subaru, but my father sitting in a foldout beach chair. He has a manila folder in his hand, which I recognize as the one containing all my old drawings from elementary school.

"I can't believe you saved those!" I notice the propane torch next to him on the workbench. "So what's with the torch? Planning on burning them before somebody discovers the truth about how sucky I was?"

"Burn them? I wouldn't do that." He uses a flint to light the torch, then uses the torch to light a joint. "Unless you want me to?" He tentatively holds the torch up to the stack of drawings.

"No!" I startle myself with how loud it comes out.

Of course, my unflappable father shows no response other than turning off the torch and tossing it back onto the workbench.

"Sorry," I apologize.

"That's alright. You know, I've been thinking about your selling-out problem."

"Come to any conclusions?"

"Yes. That it's all subjective." He offers me a hit off his joint.

"How do you mean?" I shake my head no to the joint.

"Well, it seems obvious that 'artistic vision' is a deeply personal thing, intrinsically linked to the artist who has it." He pauses, examining an old gardening clog on the garage floor.

"Okay."

"Right . . . so if you then define 'selling out' as any intentional act which goes against said artistic vision, it is necessarily subjective. What might be selling out for you—that is, a deliberate act which violates your artistic vision—might not be selling out for your new friend Mirabel Matamoros. In fact, given my *objective* observation that she most likely lacks artistic vision entirely, it may not even be possible for the stupid fucking ho-bag to sell out at all."

Stunned by my father's uncharacteristic use of profanity, it takes me a moment to recover.

"So essentially, you're saying that I have to decide for myself whether doing an ad for vaginal rejuvenation is selling out?" I ask.

"Exactly."

"I'm not sure if that helps me any."

He doesn't respond to this, and in the ensuing silence, I can't help but start thinking about how vaginal rejuvenation obviously doesn't at all fit into my artistic vision. Ever the psychological chess player, I suspect this was his intention.

"You know, your mother and I are really proud of you," he says, finally speaking again. "Being an artist has got to be one of the hardest things in the world to do."

"Thanks."

"And if you end up deciding to do the vaginal rejuvenation ads, we'll still be proud of you."

Checkmate.

• • •

Back in my bedroom, I put Jello down on the carpet and shut the door to keep Horst's puppy out. She sprints to hide under the bed, then thinking better of it, sprints again to hide in the closet. I pick up my cell phone with the vague intention of calling someone to vent to, but it occurs to me that (pathetic as it is) the only person I can really talk to at this point is Alex, and if I call him again this soon it'll raise the alert level from "needy" to "potential restraining order." I settle instead on checking my messages, but all three of them are from Dahlman—the last person I want to talk to. While I'm still staring at the phone screen trying to decide what to do, the ringtone goes off and Javier's number comes up. I consider letting it go to voice mail, but take a deep breath and answer it anyway.

"*Congratulations. You look positively stunning.*"

"Huh?" It takes me a moment to realize he's referring to the *Calendar* cover. "Why thank you, sweetie. How's the statutory rape going?"

"*Don't be like that.... Are you staying at your parents' house?*"

"What's it to you?" I'm aware that I sound like a petulant preteen, but can't seem to help myself.

"*Meet me at the bat cave, then. We need to talk.*"

"What are you doing at the cave?" By "bat cave" I know he is being literal and referring to the cave up Bronson Canyon where the campy Adam West *Batman* TV show was filmed. We used to picnic there the summer we first started dating.

"*Scouting for Mirabel's video. We want a lot of climbing.*"

"I really do have to get over to the gallery for my fabulous show.... And since when did you start scouting video shoots? I thought you were a chef."

"*Don't be like that. It's important. We need to talk.*"

"Fine." I suppose it is better to finalize the breakup in person rather than over the phone. "I'll be there in twenty minutes."

18

I park at the end of Canyon Drive, where a dirt road climbs up towards the "Hollywood" Sign. There's a low vehicle gate to block the daily stream of tourists in rental cars, as well as bright red signs forbidding anything with a motor, but to my surprise it's unlocked and wide open. It occurs to me that it must have something to do with all the fires.

Instead of the main dirt road, I cross a cement bridge over the dry wash, and start hiking up a secondary hard-packed beige dust trail that curves around and leads directly to the cave. The park is almost all native chaparral (which is why it burns so easily), and with the absence of any shade beyond three-foot brush, the path normally gives off a blinding glare. But the Santa Anas have died down since last night, and a lingering marine layer has cooled the sky into a gray coastal haze. The effect is actually quite pleasant, and with the insects and doves in the surrounding brush curiously silent, I can even hear my own footsteps.

About a hundred feet above the canyon floor, I pass a small patch of hillside (less than a quarter acre) that has turned entirely black. Everything—the brush, the manzanita, the wild sage, even the grass—has been incinerated to charcoal. It's obvious that only a lucky water drop from one of the fire helicopters saved the rest of the area from going up in smoke. I scan the sky and then listen for a moment to make sure there aren't any other fire helicopters nearby. The more I think about it, the stupider it seems to be meeting here, but I figure that if there were any real danger, the fire department would have at least put up warning signs at the park entrance.

Since the cave is entirely artificial, carved adjacent to a former quarry as a movie prop, it isn't the least bit hidden, but burrowed openly through twenty-five yards of red rock with an entrance at either end. The trail itself widens into a clearing of slightly more yellowish-beige dirt that has been bulldozed in front of the cave. While it's obvious that this cleared area is merely there to allow the equipment and trucks necessary for filming to set up in front of the cave, it has been inadvertently captured in so many movies and TV shows that it now appears as an almost natural characteristic of caves in general. Even the two perfectly shaped boulders placed with deliberate haphazardness in front of the cave's entrance would be believable if one of them hadn't been partially kicked in by vandals. Unable to resist the urge to be bionic, I walk over to the other one and lift it over my head. It's hollow fiberglass, weighing less than ten pounds.

I remember back in elementary school, I once ditched class after lunch and came down to the caves by myself to watch them film a blaxploitation movie remake that (as far as I know) never actually got released. I hid up on a ridge and watched take after take of a biker in denim firing a sawed-off shotgun at a purple Cadillac as it fishtailed its way into the cave. I stayed crouching on the ridge the whole afternoon, until they eventually ran out of blanks for the shotgun.

Tossing the boulder aside, I walk up to the cave's entrance. There are a number of rusting steel rivets jutting out of the rock, and about a foot into the cave the walls and ceiling have been painted black to make the interior darker. I call out Javier's name, and listen as it vanishes into the darkness without an echo. I hesitate. Turning away from the entrance, I eyeball the hard-packed dirt and surrounding jagged hills until my eyes come to rest on the ridge where as a child I hid to watch them filming the purple Cadillac. There's no one.

After calling his name once more, I walk a couple yards into the cave and wait for my eyes to adjust. With the exception of a few plaster animal skulls left over from some movie crew, it looks more or less like it did when I was a child. I turn around twice to survey the empty rock walls, most of which were hand-chiseled for a more authentic look. The knowledge that the cave is merely a movie prop only seems to amplify my claustrophobia, and I'm about to leave when I catch sight of something moving at the far end of the cave. My heart picks up speed.

"Hello?" I call out, trying to keep my voice steady.

"I missed you."

Javier moves into the light. Backlit by the far entrance to the cave, he looks disturbingly angelic. I walk towards him, but the expected surge of emotion fails to arrive. Nothing. No love, hate, joy, or rage.

My mind quickly flips through a Rolodex of appropriate words and actions. Everything from a war cry to a plea, from a peck on the cheek to a slap. But despite, or perhaps even because of the movie set atmosphere, I fail to feel dramatic—as if I'm watching the whole scene in Cinemascope. It's only when I'm face-to-face with him that I notice that his teeth are so white they're almost phosphorescent.

"What's with your teeth?" I finally ask.

"Huh?"

"Did you leave the bleach on too long or is that bonding?"

"Isabel . . ." He shakes his head and sighs.

"What?"

"You're just like one of those curmudgeons who writes essays for the *New York Review of Books* decrying the death of literature." His tone is so patronizing, he could be a White House press secretary.

"And that's supposed to mean... ?" I feel the emotional numbness start to ebb.

"It means, give it up, geezer. Nobody fucking reads these days anyway. Isabel, do you really think people give a shit whether or not my 'Dentaperm Next Generation porcelain veneers' are real?" He uses his fingers to emphasize the quotation marks. "Maybe if you yanked that cricket bat out of your ass you'd see that natural-looking teeth went the way of the family sitcom. But nooooooo, you have to have 'morals.'" Again he uses the quotation mark fingers. "Face it, baby, the only difference between Martin Luther King Jr. and Paris Hilton is that MLK played the race card."

There's a pause as I wait to see if "race card" gets the quotes. Apparently it doesn't.

"Javier, are you completely fucking retarded or just—"

"You trying to starve yourself?" He changes the subject by grabbing my forearm and checking its plumpness.

"Don't touch me." I jerk my arm away.

"Heroin chic is sooo mid-nineties."

"Oh, and porcelain veneers are—" My words and thoughts are silenced as Javier suddenly kisses me. I try to pull away and ask him what he's doing, but his hands reach around my hips and the words stutter in my throat. There are no pauses, no fumbles, no chances to reflect on where my T-shirt has disappeared to or how he managed to get my jeans off over my boots. I feel myself falling and brace for impact on the rock floor, only to find that Javier has put down blankets.

"You bastard," I manage to comment on his forethought.

"Those who fail to plan, plan to fail." He laughs, smiling down at me, and then moves in.

"Fuck you."

"Okay."

Five minutes later, I'm actually biting my lip not to climax so soon, but do anyway. Carried away by the artificial cinematic atmosphere, I claw at his back and notice that his love handles are gone. Even though they were barely noticeable, he'd spent the last year trying to low-carb them away to no effect.

"I really needed that." Javier rolls off and collapses next to me on the blanket.

"Did you get liposuction?" I lift his shirt above the waist and see the bruises.

"Huh?" Javier jerks the shirt back down. "You know, not everyone was born with perfect genetics."

"I don't mean to be cruel," which of course is a bold-faced lie, "but you used to have a little more ... fortitude."

"It's those fucking Sherpas. They convinced Mirabel to stop

having sex while she trains. I swear to God, it's been like two weeks."

"Sure. That must be it."

"Hey, what's with the hostility?" He leans over onto his elbow to look at me.

"I don't know . . . maybe it's the fact that you left me for a sixteen-year-old pop star who thinks Sherpas are from Switzerland?"

"You're so judgmental. You really need to deal with that." Javier shakes his head and tries to give me a condescending kiss on the forehead, but I squirm away.

"No dice, Botox boy. You can't just go off whoring with the Latina Britney Spears for two months, and expect me to take you back at the snap of a finger."

"Who said I wanted you back?" He laughs.

My fist shoots out just as he leans in for another attempt at a kiss and slams with the combined force of both our movements into his left eye socket. As a result, the impact is exaggerated to a cartoonish ***BLAM!!!*** fitting of our bat cave surroundings. Javier's head snaps back at least two feet and drags the rest of his body along with it as he flies off the blanket.

I stare with dumb awe at my knuckles for a second, then crawl over to look at a stunned Javier. The moment his one good eye focuses on me, he throws his forearm defensively in front of his face.

"Christ! *No más*!"

"Sorry, you leaned into it."

"What are you, taking Muay Thai now?"

I shrug, trying not to smile at his rapidly swelling eye. The pain from my knuckles is already radiating through the back of my hand and into my wrist, but it's surprisingly pleasant to feel something so intense.

"Help me up, would you?"

Using my uninjured left hand, I awkwardly pull him to his feet, and we both get dressed. Watching him make his unsteady way to the back entrance of the cave, I almost feel sorry for him. Almost.

"You know you deserved that, don't you?" I follow him out into the quarry proper. Squinting up at the wispy clouds and blue sky above the high rock walls, I notice that the haze is already starting to burn off. The winds have shifted again, and the warm Santa Anas are rustling the brush along the ridgeline.

He doesn't answer until he reaches the center of the quarry and stops.

"Mirabel and I are getting married in Cabo next week."

"Next *week*? Are you fucking crazy?"

"I love her, Isabel."

"She's sixteen years old! That's not even legal, for Christ's sake!"

"It is where she comes from."

"Where? Salt Lake City?"

"No, I mean her native country."

I stare at him, unable to comprehend how I could ever have been tricked into dating such a truly ridiculous human being, much less have just fucked him five minutes ago.

"Then why the hell are you here with me?"

"I told you, Mirabel won't have sex while she's training. I saw the picture of you in the paper this morning, and thought . . ."

"You'd get a farewell fuck before tying the knot?"

"It's not like that." He takes a step forward, then thinks better of it, and steps back out of punching range again. "I just thought that since technically we're still dating, it wouldn't be cheating."

I actually do consider hitting him again, but my knuckles

have swollen to the point where I can't close my fist anymore.

"Isabel, I imagine you've figured out by now that deep down I'm ... well, a very driven person. It's 'survival of the fittest' out there, and I'm playing 'Tristate Powerball.'" He's back doing the quotes with his fingers. "It's like Cesar Chavez always said: 'By any means necessary.'"

"Actually, that was Malcolm X."

"My point exactly." He tries to give me an expression, but the Botox keeps his face blank. "Mirabel and I are really perfect for each other."

I can't argue with that.

"I still love you, Isabel."

"Well then—"

I'm not sure what I was going to say, but Javier obliterates it midstream with a quick step forward and a sudden kiss. Despite everything, I feel that humiliating mute limpness coming on again. After a few feeble attempts to punch him in the kidney with my swollen hand, I resign myself to getting fucked again, and am wondering where he's hidden the blankets this time, when he surprises me by pulling away.

"I hope you'll come to the wedding." He smiles blankly.

"No fucking way."

He lifts his finger to his cheek and makes his unswollen eye larger with the same gesture the parking lot attendant and the Armenian woman made yesterday, and then disappears into the cave.

"Hey! What the hell does that eyeball thing mean, anyway?" I yell after him, but he's already gone.

I stare at the darkness of the cave for a minute, then turn back to the quarry walls.

"Arrggghhhh!!!" My scream explodes into a chaos of echoes. It's the first time I've screamed at the top of my lungs in years, and just like the pain from my swollen knuckles, it feels surprisingly good. I take a deep breath and decide to try it again. "Aacccckkkk!!!"

As if in response, a deer leaps over the lip of the quarry and starts bounding down the unbelievably steep slope. While I'm still trying to process how my scream could scare a deer two hundred yards away, a jackrabbit leaps over the lip of the quarry at the same point where the deer came down, and falls headlong to its death on the rocks below. I look up again at where it jumped from, and notice smoke and ash beginning to blow over the lip and down into the quarry.

"Javier," I mumble, then turn towards the cave and yell. "Javier! Fire!"

There's no reply. Another jackrabbit leaps to its death off the quarry wall, and then an intense red glow visible even in the sunlight crawls over the rim and scatters embers into the brush along the quarry floor. It's as if someone's fired a starter pistol. Ground squirrels, jackrabbits, and rats begin jumping out from behind every rock and shrub to charge straight at me, heading instinctively for the shortcut through the cave.

Before any conscious thought to run even occurs to me, I'm barreling along with the rest of the animals at top speed. When I make it to the other end of the cave, I find myself the slowpoke in an even larger animal exodus including coyotes, deer, skunks, and a family of opossums trying to get away from the brushfire. The ground is rocky on the hill above the cave, and without as much ground cover the fire temporarily slows, but I can see embers floating out on the wind into the heavier brush around me.

By the time I reach the first bend in the dirt road, the blaze has already crossed farther down and blocked it entirely with smoke and a ten-foot wall of flame, so I join the animals in their charge straight down the sandy slope to the dry wash at the bottom of the canyon. The brush whacks my face so violently that I'm forced to close my eyes, and within a few steps I lose my footing and begin sliding down an arroyo with panicked animals running right over me. I grab frantically at a manzanita bush, but it uproots in the sandy soil and follows me down into the wash.

The angle of the slope eases a little along the bank of the dry streambed, and I'm surprised to come to a relatively gentle halt. The animals continue running, heading down the wash towards the entrance of the park. My right ankle is twisted, and one elbow is raw and full of dirt, but I manage to get to my feet. A thick black smoke starts to fill the canyon as the sycamore trees along the wash begin to burn, and I break into a hobbled run toward the road. I'm less than ten feet away when Javier's Saab careens by, slamming into the speed bumps like moguls on a ski run. By the time I get my arms up to wave, he's already gone, barreling towards the park exit.

"You motherfucker!!!" I manage to scream, before I'm knocked flat on the ground again as the world explodes into a white cloud.

19

My mother is standing on the gallows with her hands tied behind her back while the hangman is checking the noose.

"Mom, what happened?"

"Oh, this?" She laughs. "This is just a slap on the wrist from the real estate board. They found out that I stole the plots to all my children's books from Shakespeare."

"But can they do this?"

"Actually, it would have been a whole lot worse if Armando hadn't mounted a defense to put Perry Mason to shame. He played the jury like a pinball machine. Even the court stenographer stood up and—"

The hangman puts a black hood over her head, muffling the rest of the sentence. He adjusts the noose and slips it around her neck.

"Wait!" I call out to the hangman. "How could she have stolen the plots from Shakespeare? Her books are about children colonizing the moon!"

"It's all subjective." He shrugs and releases the trapdoor.

• • •

The tremendous heat from the fire is gone, and it occurs to me in an objective way that I must be dead. This thought seems to bother me less than knowing that Dahlman will probably find some humiliating way to digitize my image posthumously and use it in an adult undergarment or hemorrhoid cream commercial. But I suppose if you die a sellout, you can't really complain about people profiting off your death.

The white mist starts to clear, and I'm surprised to find myself not just dead, but very very wet. It's only when I look up and spot the helicopter veering off overhead that I realize they must have done an emergency water drop right on top of me. Whether or not they actually saw me under all the smoke is unclear, but I make a mental note to drop to my knees and fellate the next fireman I meet.

Once again I manage to get to my feet. With my brain oozing around in my skull like a broken egg yolk and the bank now slippery with mud, I fall twice as I limp up the last ten yards to the road. Because of the trail switchback, I'm actually about a hundred yards down canyon from where my Nova is parked in the lot at the end of the paved road, so I grit my teeth at the pain from my twisted ankle and start making my way towards it. Spot fires caused by the floating embers have already caught on the far side of the canyon, and the wind at my back has picked up to a roar, but considering that what little I know about fires comes from the movie *Backdraft*, I'm not sure if it's the Santa Anas or the beginning of some sort of firestorm. The animals, of course, are still fleeing in the opposite direction, which gives me the odd sensation of moving forward at a fantastic speed, even though my crippled ankle is keeping me from hobbling at little more than a geriatric jog.

By the time I do reach the car, the heat from the fire has already dried my clothes and warmed the black Nova like an August trip to Death Valley. I frantically search for the keys, hop in the car, and (miracle car that it is) manage to get it started on the first try. Using my uninjured left foot to slam the pedal down, I speed towards the park entrance with my hand on the horn and squirrels popping under the tires.

Since the wind is blowing up canyon, the fire can't keep up with me and eventually falls behind among the houses just outside the park. However, instead of ebbing, the adrenaline driving my left foot into the gas pedal actually increases the farther I get from the actual flames, and by the time I reach Franklin Avenue, I'm swerving wildly between the lanes and sideswiping parked cars left and right. Traffic is light and the stoplights are out (either from the fire or the aftershocks), and I fishtail so hard to make the right that I pop the corner curb on the wrong side of the street and send a flock of pedestrians from the Scientology center fleeing for their lives. I floor it again and start heading west down Franklin, then change my mind and take another rubber-burning right at the next block, swerving into one of the empty diagonal spaces next to the Daily Planet newsstand and knocking the parking sign askew as I finally screech to a halt.

I try to catch my breath, but the noise is still a solid deafening wail loud enough to make my teeth hurt. It's only when I throw up my hands to cover my ears and the sound ceases abruptly that I realize I had my hand on the horn.

I drop the car into park.

Then turn the radio on.

Then quickly turn it off again and pop the car back into drive.

I fasten my seat belt, check the gas gauge, and flip the radio on and off again.

"Okay. Just calm the fuck down." Saying the words out loud seems to at least temporarily increase their effect. I kill the engine, unbuckle my seat belt again, and step out onto the sidewalk in front of the Daily Planet newsstand.

For just a moment I feel slightly dizzy, as if I've stood up too fast, and then it hits me. Black nausea claws at my temples and I suddenly buckle over to vomit into the gutter. Not just my recent brush with death at the bat cave, but all the disturbing events of the previous two days flood my mind and seem to be retching their way out of me at the same time. The remnants of *pan dulce* and *jamón* come up easily, but the subsequent dry heaves last a full five minutes, my empty stomach contracting against my emaciated back and ribs with a will of its own.

When I finally manage to stand up again, I notice a blond-haired surfer boy with beady little weasel eyes leaning against the Daily Planet magazine racks with a copy of *Artforum* in his hand. He's staring at me.

"You okay?" he asks with blasé stupidity.

"Do I look okay?" I spit into the gutter, trying to clear the vomit out of my mouth.

"Let me guess. Too much Jägermeister last night?" He laughs.

"Actually, I was up by the bat cave and almost got burned alive."

To my annoyance, this revelation has no effect whatsoever on his bong-slackened features.

"Really?" The boy pulls a bottle of Visine Tears out of his pocket and starts putting drops in his eyes. "Is that how you hurt your hand?"

"My what?" I look down with irritation at the hand I punched Javier with, and see that it's swollen like an oven mitt, not to mention bright red. "No ... but I did hurt my elbow." I try to show him the dirt-filled gash, but he's still putting in the eyedrops. I involuntarily start rubbing my own eyes, which suddenly seem to have gone excruciatingly dry.

"Huh." The eyedrops begin to roll down his cheeks, and he finally puts the Visine away. "You know." He fixes his weasel eyes on me again. "You really should smile more."

"Yeah? Well, you really should shove your head another couple inches up your ass and see if you can find your fucking brain."

Considering my inexperience with ad-libbing insults, I'm rather impressed with myself for coming up with that one. The surfer boy is temporarily struck dumb, and I limp away towards Franklin before he can make a comeback.

By the time I reach the corner, I've calmed down enough to realize that this is the sort of emergency you're supposed to report. Despite the drenching from the water drop, my cell phone takes a cue from the Nova and still works.

I dial 911.

"*Yep?*"

"Is this 911?"

"*Yep.*"

"I'd like to report a brushfire."

"*By brushfire, do you mean the unstoppable inferno that is currently racing through Griffith Park and the surrounding residential areas, remorselessly destroying everything in its path?*"

"Yes."

"*Do you really think we haven't noticed?*"

"No ... it's just—"

"Perhaps you'd also like to report yesterday's aftershocks?"

"But—"

"I'm sorry, 911 is for slightly more subtle emergencies. Thank you for calling."

The line goes dead. I stare at my cell phone, then look up at the surfer boy who's putting in *more* eyedrops. It suddenly occurs to me that my parents' house is up in the hills directly above the fire. I start speed-dialing frantically.

The home line is dead.

My mother's cell phone goes straight to voicemail.

My father's cell phone . . .

"Hello, honey."

"Dad? Are you alright?"

"Fine. And you?"

"Listen, there's a fire and . . ."

"Been there, done that. We lost the lower terrace of your mother's garden and Armando's garage got a little singed, but other than that, we're alright. There was a smoke jumper crew from Oregon. They were really something. Your mother even made them lemonade." As usual, his voice betrays not the least bit of excitement.

"Thank God. Are you at home now?"

"No, at the gallery. They ordered an evacuation. A little bit ass-backwards in my opinion, but since we were all headed down here to see the show anyway, it worked out fine."

"So everyone's okay?" I'd completely forgotten about my show.

"Well, everyone but Dahlman. He's really pissed you're not here yet. Do you want me to put him on?"

"No . . . I'll be there soon."

20

The Bourgeois Pig coffee house is right next door to the newsstand, and I figure it's as good a place as any to sit down and try to recover. The blue walls are covered with paintings by a local artist who is clearly more than a little obsessed with male genitalia, and the light coming in from a gated window facing the street gives the place a miasmal feel despite the fact that no one is smoking. The only person in the place not furiously typing away at a screenplay on his or her laptop is the barista behind the counter.

I head straight to the unisex bathroom in the back and rinse my mouth out with the rust brown water coming out of the tap. It's only after I've gargled and spit three times that I remember the radio warning to boil all tap water. I didn't swallow any, but then back in high school I once got sick just from brushing my teeth with the water in Cancún.

While I'm trying to blot the inside of my mouth dry with a paper towel, my cell phone goes off and Cordelia's name comes up (she must have programmed it in).

"Hello?"

"*Where the fuck are you?*" she asks.

"Where the fuck are you?" I counter.

"*I asked you first.*"

"I'm at the Bourgeois Pig."

"*Great, I'll be there in five minutes.*" She hangs up.

When I walk out of the bathroom, I can see the barista eyeballing me suspiciously. Since I have to wait for Cordelia anyway, I walk to the counter to buy something, and out of habit I order a latte (realizing too late that hot milk and coffee is about the last thing I want). I take the latte back over to a table by the window just as the CD player changes discs and "The Girl from Ipanema" starts to play, followed by a collective groan from the screenwriter crowd.

The steady tapping of keyboards, the slow bossa nova beat, and the soft humming of the barista behind the counter all combine to create an eerie calm. In a matter of minutes, I've gone from fleeing for my life to sitting in a café listening to elevator music. The adrenaline dump hits me at the same time I try a sip of the latte, and suddenly I'm shaking so hard it's all I can do to put down the mug without spilling. I glance around at the screenwriter crowd, but they're all too busy typing to notice. (There's something terribly ironic about a room full of aspiring screenwriters working on their "disaster" scripts, when just outside the door the world is being engulfed by wildfires.) I stare out the gated window trying to keep from crying, and watch three military Humvees drive by on their way (I suppose) to the fire. Curiously, I neither see nor hear any fire trucks. Maybe they ran out of them.

Just when I've finally stopped shaking enough to sip the now lukewarm latte, Cordelia comes charging in the door.

"Hey, you have to be eighteen to come in here," the barista calls out to try and stop her.

"Don't be such a nancy boy," Cordelia counters. "I'll be out of here before you can suck your own dick."

This seems to shut the barista up, and Cordelia comes over to sit at my table.

"Does this have real dairy in it?" She picks up my mug of latte to examine it. "That shit will kill you."

"Were you just in the neighborhood?" I ask, wondering how she could have gotten to the Pig so fast.

"No, I secretly implanted a GPS homing device in the trunk of your car when I dumped the bones in there. I've been tracking your movements all day with my laptop."

I laugh, and then realize she's serious.

"It's not that I don't trust you, it's just that I have a general lack of faith in humanity." Cordelia shrugs and lights up the stub of a Cohiba cigar.

"Hey!" the barista calls out. "That's illegal!"

"Alright! Alright!" She waves him off and drops the cigar stub in my latte.

"So did you come to get the bones back?" I ask, trying to distract her from whatever scene she's going to cause next.

"Bingo, bimbo! I need to get them down to Tijuana by tonight. I've got buyers flying in all the way from Antwerp, not to mention the …" She trails off as she starts to notice my mud-caked clothes. "What the fuck happened to you?"

"I got caught in a wildfire up at the bat cave." Without the adrenaline driving my words, I sound disturbingly matter-of-fact.

"Well, that was stupid."

"I almost died, and all you can say is that I'm stupid?"

"Hey, what's with the hostility?" Cordelia puts her hand over her heart melodramatically. "I thought we were soul sisters."

"Fuck you."

"It'll cost you fifty. A hundred if you want your salad tossed." She starts to unzip her jeans.

"Stop!" I yell too loudly, but by this point all the screenwriters have ceased typing in order to listen in anyway. "Just stop, okay?"

"Okay."

There's a pause as Cordelia zips up and sits quietly, waiting for me to go on.

"Look, it's just … " I find myself stumbling for words when I finally do speak. "Cordelia, I know how hard things have been for you lately. Alex told me. But you've gotta stop being so …"

"So what?"

"You know."

Cordelia mulls this over for a moment, then pulls a purple cocaine bullet out of her pocket and takes a snort.

"Isabel, has it ever occurred to you that maybe you've got this all backwards?"

"How so?" I can't believe I'm even listening to her.

"Well …" She switches nostrils and takes another snort. "Just look at you." Pocketing the bullet again with one hand, she gestures at my filthy clothing and bloody elbow with the other. "Is all that Vulcan logic and rationality really working out for you? I mean come on, I may be a major fuckup, but Isabel babe, you're a fucking mess."

"I . . ." I try to think of a counterargument, but the truth is, she has a point.

"Honey, a little advice from your best friend Cordy. Sometimes you gotta take the bull by the balls and squeeze." She makes a testicle-crushing motion with her hand.

21

Ten minutes later, Cordelia's somehow convinced me to lend her my Nova for the drive to Tijuana. We leave the Bourgeois Pig, but before we can make it back to the car, a National Guardsman in desert camouflage rounds the corner onto Franklin and starts heading towards us, M16 at the ready.

"Oh shit!" Cordelia yelps, and before I can stop her, she starts fleeing in the opposite direction at a dead run. With my injured ankle, I'm not going anywhere.

"Why'd she run?" The Guardsman asks as he approaches me. Not only is the guy built like a buffalo, but I can tell by his eyes that only his training is keeping him from shooting her in the back with the M16.

"Her brother died in Iraq," I lie. "Now she flips out every time she sees someone in uniform."

"That doesn't make sense."

"No, I guess it doesn't." I shrug.

The buffalo just stands there staring at me, so I try to walk past him and head back to the Nova.

"Halt!" He stops me. "All fire evacuees are being processed at the Red Cross emergency shelter." He uses his M16 to point to Cheremoya Elementary school down the block (which is actually the same elementary school I attended).

"But I'm not a fire evacuee. I don't even live here anymore."

"Sorry. But there's a chain of command in action. Until I hear otherwise, everyone gets processed."

"Look, I don't want to detour your power trip, Private . . ." I read the name off his fatigues. " . . . BIGGSON, but until they declare martial law, you can't order around civilians." I'm starting to worry that I'm never going to get to my art opening.

"It's Corporal Biggson, and martial law was declared this morning."

"Really?"

"Really." He nods.

Looking up and down the sidewalk, I see other National Guardsmen and Guardswomen directing all pedestrian traffic towards the school, so instead of continuing to argue with the buffalo, I decide to just explain the situation to someone at the shelter. I haven't been back to my elementary school since the day I graduated, and walking through the gate onto the asphalt schoolyard with all the other dazed evacuees feels less nostalgic than simply odd. There's a group of Red Cross volunteers behind a narrow folding table, and I step into the registration line with everyone else.

"Nature of evacuation?" The Red Cross volunteer has a noticeable Southern twang as well as high-waisted blue slacks that give her a bit of a marsupial paunch.

"Uh … actually, I don't really have anything to do with this. I was just trying to get to my car, but the soldiers directed me here."

"You're not." The woman shields her eyes from the sun to look at me. "Isabel Raven, are you?"

"How'd you know that?"

"Oh!" She reaches out to shake my hand, but stops herself when she sees the condition of my knuckles. "I read all about you in the paper today. I just love your work!"

"So you'll let me get out of here and go to my opening?" I'm a little conflicted about her praise.

"Yes, well … actually, that's a tad difficult right now. You see, there's a chain of command. Until the okay comes down, we really need to keep everyone here."

"So you're holding me against my will?"

"I think you'll change your mind when you try some of the food in the cafeteria. Restaurants all over the city have been donating. Seriously, try the Uzbeki dumplings—they're to die for." She points to the main building of the school. "You head through that entrance, then take a left—"

"It's okay, I used to go to school here," I stop her.

"Really? That's great!" She shows a disturbing level of enthusiasm. "Actually, first you should get those knuckles checked out." She points to the medical tent behind her.

I look down at the swollen blob that used to be my hand and realize she's probably right. Before I can make it to the tent, however, my cell phone starts playing "Uncle Fucka" again. Several of the more Bible Belt–looking volunteers give me a dirty look, so I walk over to the tetherball court to answer it.

"Hello?"

"*AHHHHHHHHH!!!*" Dahlman screams.

"Hey, Dahlman, how's it hanging?"

"Where the fuck are you?"

"I was almost burned alive in a brushfire."

"I've got three guys here with a genital herpes endorsement offer that would make you plotz, and NO GODDAMN MOTHERFUCKING ARTIST!!!"

Since apparently Dahlman isn't going to acknowledge my recent near death experience, I take a different tack.

"The superintendent of my building told me that you took some of my underwear."

For the first time ever, I seem to have temporarily derailed Dahlman's verbal freight train. I can actually hear him cracking his neck as he prepares for round two.

"*Isabel.*" His still slightly bombastic tone drops to reverential. *"Do you have any idea how rare it is to find a talent as physically attractive as you? You could be bigger than Jeff Koons."*

"Has it ever occurred to you that I might not *want* to be bigger than Jeff Koons?"

"Nonsense . . . Look at it this way. I got you booked for an interview on Charlie Rose. *It's the fucking* Tonight Show *of the arts."*

"You never answered my question." I surprise even myself by staying strong. "Why'd you steal my panties?"

There's a long pause, but this time with no neck cracking.

"*xBay,*" he finally answers.

"xBay?"

"It's like ebay, but they're more lenient on what you can put up for auction. With the L.A. Times *piece this morning, I'm getting bids in the low five figures."*

"You're selling my panties on the Internet? You are one sick fuck."

"Hey, sweetheart, if you think I'm sick, you should see what your cradle-robbing beau Javier is selling."

I hang up.

The medical tent is completely empty of patients, and there's a scramble among the three male doctors there to see which one will treat me. The winner is a fortyish bald guy with the body of a marathon runner and the neck of an ostrich.

"You look familiar." He tilts his head to examine my face. "Do I know you?"

"I don't think so." I decide not to mention the *Calendar* cover.

"How'd you bust your knuckles fleeing a fire?"

"Actually, that was boyfriend-related."

"You have a boyfriend?" He seems crestfallen.

"Not anymore. He's marrying Mirabel Matamoros."

"The Latina Britney Spears? Isn't she like sixteen?"

"Thus, the broken knuckles."

"I see." He examines my knuckles. "But lucky for you, they're not broken."

He seems very intense while working, so we don't talk as he cleans and bandages my knuckles, as well as the dirt-filled gash on my elbow.

"So do you have a place to stay?" he asks with faux nonchalance once he's finished. One of the other doctors bursts out laughing at this, and the ostrich loses his cool. "I meant, they've converted some of the classrooms."

"Thanks. But that's okay."

With the rest of the evacuees trying to reserve bed space, I fight the tide and head into the school itself. The smell of so many radically different types of food emanating from the cafeteria at the same time is somewhat sickening, so I skirt around it and slip unseen up the stairs to the empty second floor. Trying to think up a plan of escape, I find myself absentmindedly turning the knob on every classroom door, until one finally opens.

As I walk through the door, it's like stepping back in time. Immediately I recognize it as the old art room. A lack of funding forced the school to permanently close it halfway through my fifth-grade year—the Red Cross must have unlocked it to use as emergency shelter space. Both the pottery wheel and kiln are gone, but the giant crayon stubs and multicolored scraps of construction paper are still there, as well as all the yellowed drawings cramming every square inch of the wall.

In a flash, it all comes back. A gawky introverted young Isabel sneaking in her own pastels so she wouldn't have to use the clunky crayons. The windowsill where I used to sit so I wouldn't have to work by the crappy fluorescent lights. The Christian Scientist teacher with frosted hair who hated my guts because even at age eight I could draw better than her.

It dawns on me that this is the very room where I first decided that I wanted to be an artist. Not because I wanted to make a lot of money or to be famous or even to express some deep childhood angst, but simply because I enjoyed drawing. The longer I look at the rectangles of rotting brown sketchbook paper covered in brilliant hues of crayon, the more I seem to grasp that everything Dahlman's been offering me—from the cover of the *Calendar* section to the lucrative ad campaigns to the five-figure sales of my paintings themselves—is never going to come close to the primal pleasure of artistic creation.

As if in response to this thought, my cell phone goes off again and Dahlman's number comes up on the screen. I stick the phone back in my pocket unanswered, take one final look at the elementary school art up on the wall, and head downstairs.

The Red Cross workers and National Guardsmen try to stop me as I head back to the Nova, but I shove my way right past them.

22

The streets are ominously devoid of cars as I drive out on Franklin towards West Hollywood and Dahlman's gallery. Despite the smoky haze from the fires, the world seems suddenly clearer than before, and I have the odd sensation that someone's completely removed the windshield of the car.

Instead of just tunnel-visioning by the flimsy stucco walls and ever-changing storefronts, I begin to spot all the long-forgotten landmarks of my absurd childhood: the little alley behind the Best Western where I first tried and failed to lose my virginity in the cramped backseat of a Volkswagen Scirocco … the freeway underpass where I got mugged by a crackhead wearing leg warmers and a filthy white unitard, and ended up laughing so hard at his getup that he actually pistol-whipped me … even the Magic Castle (now backlit by the blaze in the hills) where I finally did lose my virginity to an apprentice magician who insisted on performing the act while wearing a straitjacket.

I think back again to Alex's Baudrillard quote about developing a "delusional approach to the world," and it suddenly occurs to me that almost everyone in LA has already done just that. Clearly the world isn't just on a "delusional course," but has long since gone stark raving mad. People experience truly ludicrous situations every day of their lives, and yet instead of confronting them, they choose to put on blinders and ignore them.

The closer I get to Dahlman's gallery, the more vivid and alive the world around me becomes, and yet at the same time, I feel increasingly estranged from the self-deluded people that populate it. It occurs to me that this bittersweet feeling of exhilarated alienation must be similar to what my father felt when his discovery of a lifetime turned out to herald the apocalypse.

23

Inside Dahlman's gallery, the atmosphere is somewhere between carnival and riot. The place is packed with at least two hundred people, and there's both a hip-hop DJ and a full bar. Not only are my paintings hanging on the walls, but life-sized cardboard cutouts of Toby's underage naked photos of me dot the room, each with a cartoon bubble asking "Have you talked to your doctor about VR?"

I spot my parents and neighbors over in the far corner near the restrooms, as well as at least fifty other people I know. Of course, with my naked cardboard likeness all over the place, even the people I don't know recognize me instantly, and I'm able to bum a cigarette off a fawning green-haired punk boy near the door. Dahlman himself is standing next to "*American Gothic* with Tom and Katie," which hangs prominently near the bar (despite being unfinished and *still wet*). After lighting up, I make a beeline straight for him, and given my new naked-celebrity status, people part like the Red Sea for me.

"Isabel, darling, you've *arrived*!" Dahlman attempts to air-kiss me, but I stop him cold with a cloud of Pura Indígena smoke. For a second his fist actually clenches, but then instead of hitting me, he turns back around to talk to an elderly woman about "*American Gothic* with Tom and Katie."

I take another drag off the cigarette.

"You're fired." The words are barely audible over the DJ and the roar of conversation, but I can see Dahlman flinch.

"What are you talking about?" He gestures with his index finger for the elderly woman to wait and turns back around.

"I'm talking about finding another gallery to show my work, and hiring a real agent for everything else."

"You can't fire me. You signed a contract."

"No I didn't."

"No?" He cracks his neck like a boxer. "Well, there was an oral contract. By the time my lawyers get through with it, it'll seem like a fucking covenant with Yahweh himself.... You know, most girls your age would be dancing around the room like Michael Flatley if they had your sudden fame and a half-million dollars in sales. Why do you have to be the one with your panties in a bunch?"

"I don't know, maybe because you're auctioning them off on xBay."

"You really don't get it, do you?" Dahlman shakes his head, then leans in so he can whisper to me. "Do you think I don't know all this is a sham? That these paintings...." He waves his hand at the canvases surrounding us " ... are total horseshit?"

The fact that Dahlman doesn't actually like my paintings has never occurred to me, and I fail with the comeback.

"Face it, Isabel, you are not a great painter, nor will you ever be a great painter." He leans in even closer, and I can smell the

Kahlúa on his breath. "You wanna know why? Because a great painter has creativity, originality, and genius—all of which you thoroughly lack." He pauses to let this sink in. "But then, the general public is not looking for creativity, originality, or genius. They are, as pathetic as you might think it is, looking for the artistic equivalent of comfort food. And you, my darling, are truly the mac-and-cheese of the visual arts." He leans back and fixes a plastic smile on his face. "So you have a choice. Either make a pantload of Sacagaweas selling your skinny little untalented ass to people who—shocking as it is to believe—are even dumber than you, or go broke while some other hack artist dishes out the tuna noodle casserole."

Dahlman suddenly turns back to the elderly woman, and with a fake laugh continues their conversation as they walk to another painting. Up to this point, my thoughts had been focused merely on confronting him, but now something in me snaps. *Mac-and-cheese?* In some unconsciously learned cinematic gesture, my hand drops the cigarette and reaches for the nonexistent holster and six-gun on my belt. However, instead of a gun, it finds the fossilized talon that Cordelia gave me sticking out of my front pocket. Gripping the talon with my still functional left hand, I start towards Dahlman, only to have him finish talking to the elderly woman and disappear into the crowd, oblivious to my homicidal intentions.

I'm momentarily defeated, but then a serendipitous clearing in the crowd gives me a head-on view of "*American Gothic* with Tom and Katie" and I think of an even better way to hurt Dahlman than simply ripping out his jugular. I walk straight up to the painting, hook the talon into the top right corner of the canvas, and pull. The taut paint and fabric give easily, and a diagonal gash fringed with bone white gesso opens up, splitting both the painting and the couple in two. There's a gasp from the crowd around me, but Dahlman is still distracted on the other side of the room, and it takes a minute before he realizes what I've done.

"Jesus fuck!" He starts running towards me.

I'm twenty feet closer to the exit than he is, but with a twisted ankle, I barely make it to the street ahead of him. The sunlight outside the dimly lit gallery is blazing, and I falter.

"You bitch!" He explodes through the door behind me and grabs me in a chokehold. "I'm gonna fucking kill you!"

I wrestle and swing my left arm back in a feeble effort to stab him with the talon, but it hooks on his belt loop and wrenches out of my hand. Not only is the chokehold tight, but he's putting all his weight into it, causing my legs to buckle and my head to feel like it's going to pop clean off my body. Realizing that he really is trying to kill me triggers a final desperate spike of adrenaline, and I stomp my heel down on his foot.

"Uunnghh!" Dahlman lets out a simian grunt and relaxes his hold just enough for me to get a few ragged breaths in, but the blood supply to my brain is still cut off, and things start to go dark around the edges of my vision … curiously, instead of my life passing before my eyes, I see Mirabel Matamoros driving by in a tricked-out Cadillac Escalade. She's pointing at me and shouting something, but with the blood roaring in my ears, I can't hear what it is.

24

I'm back at Alex Tzu's house standing next to the L-shaped bar. *In the center of the room, Tom Cruise and Katie Holmes sit at a folding table playing poker with a tarot deck. As I approach, Tom shuffles, cuts the deck, and hands me a card. I flip it over and see that instead of a card, it's actually a free pass to a test screening of the new* Eiger Sanction *remake. I look up at him for an explanation, but he just smiles.*

"I'm sorry I destroyed your painting," I say.

"You had my eyes all wrong anyway." Tom shrugs, then points to a door I hadn't noticed in the corner of the room.

The door is smaller than it at first appears, and I'm forced to duck down almost to my knees in order to get through the frame and into the circular stairwell it leads to. The stairs are concrete and spiral up between whitewashed walls that give off the strong damp salt smell of the sea. I go up for what seems like several stories, until I come to a small landing where La Brea Woman stands in a buckskin skirt waving excitedly. Before I can say anything, she comes over and gives me a hug.

"You've always been like a sister to me."

"I have?"

"Okay, so maybe that's a bit much." She steps back. "Maybe more like cousins."

I notice that blood is streaming out of a hole in the side of her skull.

"What happened to you?"

"Mammoth stepped on my head." She giggles, then suddenly turns serious. Raising her right index finger to her right eye, she makes the same warning gesture the parking lot attendant at Musso's, the Armenian woman at the tar pits, and Javier have made.

"What does that mean?" I ask.

"Fuck if I know, but it is kind of ominous, isn't it?"

I continue up the stairs for another three or four stories until the end, and find myself looking up at a tarnished brass trapdoor in the ceiling. A thick ring handle hangs down, and when I reach up and turn it, the door unlocks and a pulley mechanism in the room above lowers another staircase. The bottom step is still a good four feet above the floor, so I have to jump and use my arms to pull myself up and out of the stairwell.

As soon as I stand, a wave of vertigo hits me so strongly that I grab onto a table to keep from falling back through the open trapdoor. The room is octagonal, with floor-to-ceiling windows on each side looking out over a vast sea of tar. When my balance returns, I inch over to one of the windows and look down. Several hundred feet below, I can see the jagged island rock on which the tower I'm in is standing. I go from window to window, but each one reveals the same impossible black expanse.

"Bravo! You finally made it." A voice comes from behind me, and I spin around to see Cordelia. "Took you long enough."

"What are you doing here?"

"I'm God."

"Huh?"

"Hey, you think I asked for the job?"

"You're God?"

"Trust me. The whole omnipotent thing? It's a crock of shit. This stuff. . . ." She points out the window at the tar. " . . . goes way over my head."

"I don't understand. . . ."

"Join the club." Cordelia takes a swig of cognac from the bottle in her hand. "Got any questions?" She offers me the bottle.

"Questions?" I shake my head no at the bottle.

"How many angels fit on the head of a pin? Is masturbation really a sin? When I die, am I going to be cast into the sulfurous fires of hell for eternity? That sort of thing."

"I . . . I don't know where to begin. . . ."

"Good, then don't. I'll just tell you the one thing I know that could possibly make a difference." She waves the cognac in my direction again. "You sure you don't want a snort?"

"No thanks."

"Where were we?"

"You were going to tell me the one thing that might make a difference."

"Yeah, now I remember." She takes another swig.

"Well? What is it?"

"This is only a dream."

25

I awake to the overpowering smell of disinfectant and for a terrifying moment wonder if Jacques Bonard isn't in bed with me. When I open my eyes, I discover with comparative relief that I'm actually in a hospital.

"Honey! You're awake!" My mother leans in and gives me a kiss on the cheek.

As my eyes start to focus, I find that not only my mother and father, but Vanessa, Armando, and Horst are all crammed in the small hospital room, watching a live freeway car chase on the TV.

"What . . . what happened?" I manage to croak.

"Dahlman was choking you."

"I mean, after that."

"Mirabel Matamoros shot him."

"What?" I try to sit up, and my mother uses the controller to raise the hospital bed.

"A nine-millimeter to the jaw, but apparently it then ricocheted up into his skull somewhere."

The car being chased on TV scrapes against a metal guardrail and casts off a shower of sparks. Everyone watching it cheers, and my mother turns to look.

"Wait . . . that's crazy, why would she shoot Dahlman?" I ask.

"She was aiming for you." My mother turns back from the TV. "Aunt Vanessa heard her scream something along the lines of 'Die, you skanky *maricoña*!' before she opened fire from an SUV."

"Where is he?"

"In surgery. You should see what was leaking from his ear—we're talking gray matter. Even if he does live, it's veggie city for sure."

The car on TV pulls an insane U-turn and starts heading back in the wrong direction on the freeway, forcing the patrol cars chasing it to swerve out of the way. Another cheer goes up from everyone in the room, and it finally dawns on me that the car is the same Cadillac Escalade that Mirabel was driving when she shot at me.

"What the hell is she doing?" I ask.

"Pulling an O.J., apparently. She's got Javier in there with her, but it's unclear whether he's a hostage or not." As if to confirm my mother's statement, the helicopter TV camera zooms in on the windshield, and sure enough, Javier is in the passenger seat—an incongruous combination of frantic gesticulations and Botoxed tranquillity. "They've been driving around the city for hours now. She's gotta run out of gas soon."

Before I can respond, the muffled sound of *South Park*'s "Uncle Fucka" fills the room, and my father reaches into his pocket to pull out my cell phone and answer it. He chats with someone for a minute or so, then covers the receiver and turns to me.

"The Whitney Biennial! Not bad." He goes back to chatting with whoever's on the other end.

I turn to my mother for an explanation.

"It's the fourth museum show offer you've gotten in the past hour. The Reina Sofía in Madrid, the Walker in Minneapolis, that one in Amsterdam . . . you've hit the big time, honey."

"So you're saying that by firing Dahlman and destroying my best painting, I've somehow managed to actually advance my career?"

"Well, it was less that than Mirabel's whole drive-by thing. It's the lead story on CNN."

26

An hour later (and against the doctor's recommendation), I'm back in the Nova headed for my apartment. I punch through the preset radio stations, but now they've switched from the prerecorded emergency broadcasts to breaking news reports about Javier and Mirabel Matamoros (who are currently stuck in traffic on the Ventura Freeway). My cell phone goes off, and despite my inferior multitasking skills, I answer it while still driving.

"Hello?"

"Sorry I missed your opening. I … well, it's a long story. Did everything go alright?" Alex asks.

"I almost died in a brushfire, then Dahlman tried to choke me to death, then Mirabel Matamoros tried to shoot me in a drive-by, then I got an offer to be in the Whitney Biennial."

"Three near-death experiences and a Whitney show in one day? Now that's just grandstanding." He laughs.

"Well, you know me. Ever the drama slut." I find myself laughing too, and despite the soreness of my bruised neck, it feels good.

"*So where are you now?*"

"I'm headed back to my apartment . . . or what's left of it."

"*Great, I'll meet you there in five minutes.*"

"Don't tell me you've got a GPS tracking device on me too?"

"A *what?*"

"Never mind."

When I arrive at the San Maximón Arms, I'm surprised to see the building looking almost level again, but one story shorter. Chris and another man are sitting on the sidewalk in beach chairs drinking Tecate from a Styrofoam cooler and smoking. Chris is wearing a Ramones T-shirt, and since it's the first time I've ever seen him out of his blue work jumpsuit, it takes the facial recognition circuits in my brain a moment to positively identify him.

"Chris?"

"Hey, Isabel! Your show was fantastic! Sorry we had to leave before you got there." The man sitting next to him nods in agreement and I realize they must be friends.

"Thank you. I don't suppose I could bum a smoke?"

"Just be careful where you toss the butt. This tar burns like a crêpe suzette." He taps out a Pura Indígena and holds the pack out for me to take it. "Some rich guy in Hancock Park blew up half a block when he tossed a Havana into the storm drain . . . I really should just quit, but I think that methane gas must have seeped into my pores. If I'm not smoking, I smell tar everywhere."

I light my cigarette off his kitchen match and take a deep drag. To my surprise, it doesn't make me the least bit faint.

"Hey, I wanted to ask you something. Is that Dahlman guy really your father? Or like your stepfather? Because I met this other guy at the gallery, a physicist, who also claimed to be your father."

"No, Dahlman's definitely not my father."

"That's a relief, because he was really a dick to Doug. Spilled Kahlúa all over his khakis and didn't even apologize."

"Who's Doug?"

"Doug Esposito? My boyfriend?" Chris introduces the man sitting with him.

"You're gay?" I'm so stunned by the idea that I blurt out the question before I can stop myself. Fortunately he laughs instead of taking offense.

"Duh."

"Wow, my gaydar needs some serious retuning." I start to reach my right hand out to shake Doug's, but remember how swollen it is just in time, and shake awkwardly with my left instead. On closer examination, he looks like a Latino near doppelgänger of Chris, complete with the tapirlike nose. "Nice to meet you."

"Charmed. Chris talks about you so much, I feel like I practically know you."

"Me too," I equivocate.

"So why are you back here?" Chris asks, trying to change the subject.

"No clue," I answer after a moment's thought.

"Well, if there's anything else you want to grab from your apartment, I'd do it now. The building's sinking at about an inch an hour."

"Is it safe to go in?"

"Fuck no."

• • •

With the entire first floor now subterranean, it's easy to jimmy open the second-floor window of my kitchen and climb inside. Everything's fallen out of the cabinets and the floor is littered with shattered plates and glasses, but I manage to make my way into the living room and grab the one remaining blank twelve-by-nine-inch canvas, a couple of brushes, some turpentine, and the toppled easel off the floor. I'm about to gather up some tubes of paint, too, when I catch sight of the empty coffee can that used to hold my brushes and have an idea.

I juggle all the stuff I'm holding so that I can pick up the coffee can too, and make my way back through the kitchen window and out to the sidewalk. There's a rivulet of tar running from a crack in the curb into the gutter, and I use it to fill the coffee can. Chris and Doug watch with half-drunk curiosity as I then thin the tar with turpentine and set up the easel with the blank canvas.

"*Oye*," Doug calls out to me, and points to the left rear easel leg, which is starting to sink into the tar on the grass. At the same time, he uses the index finger of his other hand to pull down his cheek and make his eye look larger in the same gesture everyone keeps giving me.

"What the hell does that eyeball thing mean, anyway?" I ask, readjusting the easel leg back onto the sidewalk.

"It means '*Mucho ojo*,' or 'Keep an eye out.' People use it all the time in Mexico," Doug explains.

"You'd think someone could have just told me."

"What do you mean?"

"Nothing." I shake my head, too tired to explain. Out of the corner of my eye, I spot the purple VW microbus I saw at Alex's house the night of the party pull onto the block. It drives straight up to us and double-parks across the street. Since their beach chairs are facing the apartment building, Chris and Doug have to crane their necks around to see what I'm looking at.

"Well, isn't this a Norman Rockwell moment." Alex climbs out of the driver's side carrying a silver platter covered in aluminum foil. "Gathering' round to watch the old apartment building sink into a giant toxic asphalt seep."

"Beer?" Realizing that he's a friend of mine, Chris tosses him a can of Tecate.

"Much obliged." Alex cracks the can, then walks around to the passenger side to let Cordelia out. It's only when she shuffles her way around the front of the microbus and into view that I notice she's dressed in an orange jumpsuit and shackled like a death row inmate—not just hands and feet, but with an additional chain running down the front to connect the hand and foot shackles. Throw in a face mask, and she'd look like Hannibal Lecter.

"What's with the chains?" I ask.

"It's just easier this way." Alex shakes his head as they shuffle over to our side of the street.

I turn to Cordelia to get her response, but there's a surprising lack of protest.

"Can somebody at least beer me?" She half collapses/half sits next to the cooler and tries unsuccessfully to bob for a Tecate like it's an apple. Doug finally takes pity on her and opens one so she can lie prostrate on the ground and clumsily slurp at it.

"Again, why is she in chains?" I repeat to Alex.

"Well, if you must know, she somehow managed to trick the acting assistant docent into letting her walk out of the Page Museum with a priceless collection of extinct animal bones." Alex takes the foil off the silver platter of deviled eggs he's been holding and starts handing them out to everyone. "I offered to build the museum a new hundred-million-dollar wing—you know, to grease the wheels of justice—and they said they'd drop the charges if she just tells them where she hid the bones she stole. But being a typically stubborn teenager, she won't talk."

"They're in the trunk of my car." I grab one of the deviled eggs off the platter and hand him the keys to the Nova.

"That's . . . convenient." He raises an eyebrow, then takes one of the deviled eggs himself.

"You bitch!" Cordelia makes a dramatic, but futile attempt to bite my ankle, then gives up and goes back to slurping her beer.

I fish a beer out of the cooler for myself and crack it open. The sun dips below the smoke line in the west and bathes the whole city in an otherworldly reddish light. Everything—from the low stucco buildings to the parked cars to the concrete squares of sidewalk—starts to give off a warm, almost tangible glow, until even the hideous pink stucco blob of the San Maximón Arms looks somehow beautiful as it slowly descends into the tar-dappled crabgrass. The wind off the desert falls still, and a strange quiet sets upon us all, broken only by the gentle clinking of Cordelia's chains and the muted rush of traffic in the distance.

I put down my beer, dip a brush into the tar-filled coffee can with my still functional left hand, and begin to paint.

ACKNOWLEDGMENTS

I'd like to thank the following: Jim "My Agent" McCarthy for his general (not to mention specific) fabulousness. Lisa "Tri-fold" Dahl for serving as my artistic consultant, as well as spending her valuable subway time reading something like forty drafts of this book. Miriam "The Merciless" Feuerle for her unique brand of Teutonic criticism. Jessica "Goin'" Norton for a lifetime of literary mentorship and inspiration. My parents for not giving up on what even I thought was a lost cause. Joelle Yudin, Kate Nintzel ... Oh, and some chick named Elizabeth.

About the author

About the book

Read on

Insights, Interviews & More . . .

About the author

Meet Jonathan Selwood

Courtesy of the author

Jonathan Selwood—evil incarnate or poseur extraordinaire?

I WAS BORN in Hollywood, California. In other words, the first time I played doctor as a kid was on a neighbor's circular fur-covered waterbed with a mirror on the ceiling. The girl's parents and two younger siblings were busy out by the pool hosting a nude cocaine party.

My own parents, in contrast, were from back east, and did not partake in nude cocaine parties. I was thus instilled from a young age with a strong New England–style Puritan ethic, while at the same time being raised in what is arguably the most depraved and wantonly hedonistic neighborhood in the world. When I finally graduated high school and left to attend college in Vermont, I was completely ill-prepared for the relative lack of debauchery (i.e., the nude parties had no cocaine, and the cocaine parties had no nudity).

“My own parents, in contrast, were from back east, and did not partake in nude cocaine parties.”

After college, I moved down to Chiapas, Mexico, and tried my best to write on the cheap. It lasted about four months. Then I moved to New York City and tried my best to write on the expensive. It lasted about five years. Eventually I moved to Portland, Oregon, in search of a happy medium.

Portland's been pretty good to me so far, but I must admit that in the dead of a rainy winter, I'm still inclined to wax nostalgic for those carefree sunny southern California days, and the nude cocaine parties of my youth.

“I realize your son has no legs, sir, but I'm afraid his insurance plan doesn't cover wheelchairs. Have you considered duct-taping him to some sort of a skateboard?”

Age: 27 (give or take any number of years)

Height: 4 foot 8 inches (seated)

Weight: Enough to throw around

Politics: Lapsed Anarchist

Religion: Evangelical Absurdist

Sport: Shot put

Hobbies: Talking very loudly when intoxicated, composting kitchen scraps, excessively rolling my R's when ordering bu*rrrrrr*itos . . . using ellipses . . .

Favorite Movie: Without bourbon, *Lost in Translation.* With bourbon, *The Good, the Bad, and the Ugly.*

Favorite Album: *El Poder de New York* by Oro Solido

Worst Job: HMO medical equipment denial guy (i.e., “I realize your son has no legs, sir, but I'm afraid his insurance plan doesn't cover wheelchairs. Have you considered duct-taping him to some sort of a skateboard?”)

Best Job: Writer ▶

Meet Jonathan Selwood ***(continued)***

Strangest Job: Bouncer at a bar in Chiapas, Mexico. Despite growing up in Los Angeles, my knowledge of Mexican slang is limited at best. I often resorted to waving a baseball bat in the air and screaming things like, "I throw feces at your slatternly granddaughter's chicken tamales, you obese pubic hair!"

Best Drink I Ever Invented: The Eyeball. (Two ounces Everclear, two ounces water, ice, and three dashes Angostura bitters. *Why yes, it* is *strong . . .)*

Worst Drink I Ever Invented: The Exxon Valdez. (Two ounces Kahlua, two ounces Jagermeister. Garnish with an anchovy.)

A Conversation with Jonathan Selwood

In this era of global terrorism and unchecked celebrity proliferation, do you feel that writing fiction is more or less equivalent to drinking your own urine?

No.

I notice you write on a "computer."

Yes.

Do you ever feel guilty about the fact that writing for you is little more than tapping away effortlessly at a keyboard, while there are writers in developing countries who are reduced to smearing their prose in human filth across the bathroom wall?

Which countries are you talking about?

Liechtenstein, for one.

Then my answer would have to be no.

Next question. Isn't it true that you were once forcefully ejected from a Chicago KFC after repeatedly stabbing your own testicles with a plastic spork?

Define "forcefully."

"Against your will."

Then again, my answer would have to be no. I had every intention of leaving . . . eventually. ▸

"Isn't it true that you were once forcefully ejected from a Chicago KFC after repeatedly stabbing your own testicles with a plastic spork?"

A Conversation with Jonathan Selwood
(continued)

Last question. I read in your Wikipedia entry that you are the illegitimate great grandnephew of legendary American writer and humorist Mark Twain. Is this true?

I'm very glad you asked that question. The answer is no.

Interviewer Djawn Cellwüde is coauthor of the soon-to-be self-published prose-poetry collection *God Bless Jesus!*, as well as a tireless campaigner for men's reproductive rights.

Tar and Bones

An Earlier Draft of *The Pinball Theory of Apocalypse*

I STARTED THIS NOVEL by penning what seemed like a brilliant idea for the final scene: a young girl in the rain drops an unopened letter from her dead mother into the gutter, then watches it float down the block and into a storm drain. It was only after writing the entire first draft of the book that I realized this "Dead Mother in the Gutter" scene was an absolute shitburger. I promptly shredded the only copy and buried it with some kitchen scraps in the backyard compost pile.

Over the years, I must have used ten different working titles for the book, as I obsessively rewrote draft after draft. Draft three was a total bloodbath—I actually had the protagonist, Isabel Raven, wielding a sawed-off elephant gun. Draft four had all the prehistoric animals in the La Brea tar pits come back to life and charge down Hollywood Boulevard. And it wasn't until draft five that I realized the book was actually a comedy.

You think I'm fucking with you, don't you?

Well, I'm not. Check out this third-person excerpt from an earlier draft titled *Tar and Bones:*

"Hey!" Cordelia's voice came from up on the observation deck. "You're not shooting anyone before I kill you!"

Both Isabel and Alex looked up to see her standing next to a still shirtless Dahlman. She had on a three-quarter-length leather jacket that Isabel recognized as Dahlman's and was ▸

"Draft three was a total bloodbath—I actually had the protagonist, Isabel Raven, wielding a sawed-off elephant gun."

Tar and Bones *(continued)*

awkwardly shouldering an enormous double-barrel goose gun.

"That doesn't make any sense." Alex cocked his head to one side. "How can I shoot someone after I'm dead?"

"My point exactly." Cordelia leaned her forearm on the observation deck railing and took aim.

"Wait! Wait!" Isabel held up her hand to stop Cordelia. "He just said he wasn't planning on shooting me. So you don't have to kill him."

"Stand aside, Isabel." Cordelia waved her away with her trigger hand. "This has got nothing to do with you. That greasy little architect killed my father."

"Jacques? He didn't kill Jacques. Javier did." Isabel pointed before realizing the implication.

"Oh?" Cordelia shifted the barrels around to aim at Javier.

While everyone was distracted, Javier had finished reloading the revolver and was just slamming the cylinder back in the frame.

"Like father, like daughter!" he yelled and took aim.

Compared to the pistol shots fired before, the explosion from Cordelia's shotgun thundered like field artillery, echoing off the museum walls, and sending her stumbling back from the rail. Isabel switched her attention to Javier just in time to see his head explode—brains, bone, and blood flying in one direction, while the fake beard skewed off in the other, arced through the air, and landed at her feet.

"Jesus!" everyone but Isabel yelled in consolidated awe.

Javier's revolver arm suddenly swung

“‘That doesn't make any sense.' Alex cocked his head to one side. ‘How can I shoot someone after I'm dead?'”

around to point straight up at the sky, and despite his almost complete decapitation, managed to fire all six rounds into the air before collapsing.

For a full minute they all stared dumbly at his body until Alex broke the silence.

"He's like one of those fucking chickens with its head cut off!"

"You killed him!" Dahlman's voice cracked up an octave to that of an adolescent boy's.

"Christ, Cordelia, what the hell kind of gun is that, anyway? A one gauge?" Alex walked over to examine the body. "Everything above the waist is chopmeat!"

"Vengeance is mine." Cordelia leaned the goose gun against the railing and started rubbing the spot where the wooden butt had slammed into her shoulder. "Honey," she kissed Dahlman on the cheek, "you don't have any cigarettes left in here, do you?"

"I . . . wait." Dahlman tried to stop her before she reached into the pocket of his three-quarter-length leather coat that she was wearing, but her hand had already found something.

"What's . . ." Cordelia pulled out a pair of black cotton panties. "What's . . . What the fuck is this shit? These aren't mine!"

"Wait . . . I can . . ." Dahlman started backing away from her.

"Whose are these?" Cordelia threw them at Dahlman and grabbed the shotgun.

"They're Isabel's. But it's not what you think. It's, it's really just a—" He reached the stairs and turned to make a run for it, but Cordelia had already braced the butt of the shotgun against the rail and fired the second barrel into the small of his back. ▶

"'You killed him!' Dahlman's voice cracked up an octave to that of an adolescent boy's."

Tar and Bones **(continued)**

Despite his weight, Dahlman was lifted completely off his feet and soared at least five feet, before somersaulting over and landing head first into the concrete at the bottom of the stairs.

"Ouch. That's gotta hurt." Alex winced.

Cordelia brought the gun back to her shoulder and spun around to point it at Isabel.

"Die! You back-stabbing middle-aged bitch!" She yanked at the trigger several times before realizing both barrels had already been fired. "Goddamnit!" Cordelia tossed the shotgun into the Lake Pit.

"You tried to kill my daughter!" Alex waved the Glock at her.

"She stole my boyfriend!"

"He stole my underwear," Isabel chimed in matter-of-factly.

"I trusted you, Cory." Alex shook his head. "I've been buying drugs from you and your family for over thirty years, and this is how you treat me? By trying to kill what is as far as I know my only daughter?"

"I didn't shoot! The gun was empty!"

"Say goodbye, you little slut." He took aim with the Glock.

Seriously, perhaps the only thing that remained a constant throughout all the drafts was my desire to write a book that could be read in one sitting. I wanted *The Pinball Theory of Apocalypse* to be the kind of novel you start while the plane pulls away from the jetway at LAX, and finish just as you land in New York—a quick intense read with no mid-novel logorrhea to slog through and make you wish you'd rented the crappy headset.

“I wanted *The Pinball Theory of Apocalypse* to be the kind of novel you start while the plane pulls away from the jetway at LAX, and finish just as you land in New York.”

A Reading Group Guide

1) Did anyone bother to actually read the book, or should we just start in on the Pinot Gris?
2) Do you consider yourself a media whore? Do you secretly wish you were?
3) Given the recent loss of everything we hold sacred, is Selwood's unique brand of dark comedy the only form of fiction that really matters anymore?
4) Stuck on a desert island, would you do Javier?
5) Stuck in an airplane bathroom, would you do Isabel?
6) Seriously, did anyone else notice that all the main characters' descriptions match those of animals excavated from the tar pits?
7) How many of you over the legal age of eighteen have sent smutty photos of yourselves reading *The Pinball Theory of Apocalypse* to the author? (Author's Note: Please please please . . .)
8) Let's have a show of hands. Have *you* talked to your doctor about VR?
9) What kind of lazy-assed son of a bitch takes his author photo in the bathroom mirror?
10) Fuck Pinot Gris. Let's do shots.
11) Stuck in an airplane bathroom on a desert island, would you do me?
12) Is this Isabel Raven chick for real? (www.isabelraven.com)
13) Who's cuter, Scarlett Johansson or Jessica Alba? ▶

“Did anyone else notice that all the main characters' descriptions match those of animals excavated from the tar pits?”

A Reading Group Guide ***(continued)***

14) Who's hornier, Charlie Sheen or Tommy Lee?
15) What the hell is an "ass clown" anyway?
16) Fuck Selwood. Let's spark up a fatty and watch *Battlestar Galactica.*

"What the hell is an 'ass clown' anyway?"

Vaginal Rejuvenation
Is It Right for You?

Selwood
Labiatric
Institute of
Technology

Read on

In an image-conscious world where plastic surgery has become commonplace, our staff of medically trained doctors provides you with the uncommon touch *where it counts.* A recent informal study of Harvard University undergraduates revealed that nine out of ten women feel at least some level of embarrassment when their genitals are suddenly exposed in a public setting. Why? They suffer from VDD, or in what's known in layman's terms as Vaginal Dysmorphic Disorder.

Until recently, there was little a VDD sufferer could do beyond keeping her genitals fully covered at all times. But through extensive surgical trial and error, we here at the Selwood Institute have managed to randomly combine various cutting-edge vaginal rejuvenation procedures into something that may very well be a cure for VDD. We call it a "package."

Starlet Package™

Girls as young as thirteen can safely undergo these basic procedures—

remember, you're never too young to start looking good *where it counts.* Think of the Starlet Package™ as a luxurious day at the spa for your genitals (followed by a mere six to eight weeks of activity-reduced recovery time). From the backseat of your boyfriend's car to the Hollywood casting couch of your dreams, the Starlet Package™ will give you the confidence you need to drop those drawers at the drop of a hat.

- **Laser interior/exterior hair removal**
- **Labial microdermabrasion**
- **Vulval chemical peel**
- **Bulgarian deep tissue massage**

Comeback Package™

Has your boyfriend/husband recently packed up and left? Have you been passed over for promotion at work? Did you fail to get that part in the new movie/television show you just tried out for (despite having "nailed it" in audition)? Are you over the age of twenty-three? Then perhaps it's time to consider the Comeback Package™. In this enlightened age of internet pornography, men have come to expect a level of professionalism *where it counts*, and a trip to Victoria's Secret just isn't going to cut it. As they say in the world of macro vaginal photography, twenty is the new forty. In many cases, we can actually restore your vagina to an idyllic state of prepubescent splendor. All you'll have to do is unzip that fly, and we practically guarantee your lover and/or employer will be "coming" back for more. (Three to four month recovery time.)

All the benefits of the Starlet Package™ plus:

- **Labial and/or clitoral trimming**
- **Perineum shortening**
- **Reduction of vaginal wall circumference**

Basic Instinct II Package™

Are you over the age of thirty? Or have you—gulp—had a baby or two? Well ladies, this is the package for you. You'll hike up your skirt with pride, knowing that your "ride" has been fully "pimped out." What good are a face-lift, liposuction, breast implants, and a nose job if you're not fully squared away *where it counts*? Combining traditional Western medicine with radically invasive techniques developed in the former Soviet Republic of Turkmenistan, the Basic Instinct II Package™ is sure to give you the confidence you so sorely lack. (Eight months to a year recovery time.)

All the benefits of the Comeback Package™ plus:

Vaginal Rejuvenation *(continued)*

- **Rectal tightening**
- **Laser clitoral resurfacing**
- **Liposuction of the mons pubis**
- **Hymenoplasty**

Have you talked to your doctor about VR?

Acclaimed artist Isabel Raven has!

Visit our Web site to read Isabel's story and how choosing the right S.L.I.T. package helped her career explode *where it counts.*

www.jonathanselwood.com

While a rejuvenated vagina is truly a priceless commodity, our price list is available upon request.

* Side effects are generally mild to severe, and may include partial numbness, incontinence, anal leakage, loss of sex drive, temporary paralysis, long-term paralysis, and death.